SAM CRESCENT

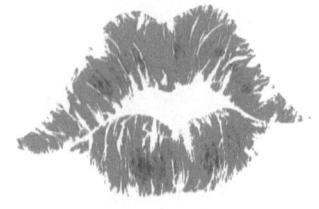

EVERNIGHT PUBLISHING ®

www.evernightpublishing.com

RIPPER'S TORMENT

Copyright© 2017

Sam Crescent

Editor: Karyn White

Cover Artist: Sour Cherry Designs

Jacket Design: Jay Aheer

ISBN: 978-1-77339-374-2

SAM CRESCENT

DEDICATION

First, as always, I want to thank Evernight Publishing and Karyn White for their constant support, advice, and help when it comes to these books. They mean so much to me that I want them to be the best they can be.

Also, a big thank you to all the readers out there for your wonderful comments and support. I really can't find the right words to express my thanks to you all.

Chaos Bleeds and The Skulls are two series that have taken me by surprise. Writing each book takes me on an emotional journey and it's not always an easy one. Judi and Ripper's book had to be done this way. The only man, in my opinion, good enough for Judi was Ripper.
I hope you all enjoy their story as much as I enjoyed writing it.

SAM CRESCENT

RIPPER'S TORMENT

Chaos Bleeds, 2

Sam Crescent

Copyright © 2014

Chapter One

Ripper gunned his machine. He shouldn't be fucking riding given how much alcohol he'd consumed, but there was no getting away from helping Princess. Judi had been officially adopted by his president, Devil, but everyone within Chaos Bleeds referred to her as Princess. She was their princess, the club princess, and no one messed with her without starting a war with the club. They all cared about her and would do anything to protect her.

Checking the name of the road, he broke the speed limit trying to get to her. Judi should be back at Devil and Lexie's party, not along some dirt road where she could get fucking murdered. Didn't women have any regard for their own personal fucking safety? He was getting pissed just thinking about her all alone. What the fuck was she doing out of the house? In fact, if she didn't have a good enough excuse he was putting her over his knee and slapping her ass silly for putting her life in danger. Didn't she know how important she was to them?

These roads were not safe for any kind of woman, not even the Chaos Bleeds Princess. He wouldn't even leave a whore to sell her wares down this strip of road. All kinds of fuckers were traveling down this road, intent on harming those weaker. He saw her standing on the embankment, pacing up and down. Ripper drew his bike close to her. The light shining over her showed the copious amounts of blood smeared over the front of her body. *Princess, what the fuck?*

Climbing off his bike, he went to her. She was crying, the tears streaking her face.

"What the fuck did you do?" He went to her, holding her at arms' length where there were no streaks of blood. Checking her over he saw none of the blood was hers.

"He wouldn't let go, and I couldn't get him to stop. Please, Ripper, I need your help."

She was sobbing. The tears poured out of her eyes with every second that passed. Cursing, he stared past her shoulder to see the car with the inside light still on. The sight made him feel sick as he knew some of what was about to come. He couldn't be mad at her for too long. Judi was a real sweetheart, and he'd seen her get stronger since Devil adopted her. They had all tried to make her leave her past behind. There was more to her than being forced to be a prostitute.

"Show me," he said, speaking gently.

Ripper followed behind her heading toward the car. Moving toward the passenger side, he saw the mess that met him. He'd caused a lot of death in his years, and the sight before him didn't affect him one bit.

"What happened?" he asked, already thinking of the men he could call to help clean this up.

"I was walking, and he told me to get into the car. I refused, and he stopped the car. I started running, and he grabbed me. I tried to get away, Ripper. I promise. I tried to fight, but he was too strong. He picked me up and dumped me in the car. I couldn't get out of the car. If I attacked him while he drove he could get us both killed. I didn't want to die. He parked here, and I freaked out." She stopped, lifting her hand to wipe the tears then stopped when she saw the blood on her hands. "He was an old customer, or at least that's what he said, along with a lot more shit." Her lips wobbled. "I somehow got out, and he grabbed me, calling me everything I can imagine."

From the sight in front of him, Ripper knew what happened. Judi had lost her temper, panicked, and shot a bullet into the man's head. He stared at the man's face lying just outside of the door. From the state of her clothing, she'd tried to hold his head but failed. Shit, he shouldn't have given her a gun. Devil was going to fucking kill him.

"Shit, I've got to get this sorted and you out of here." Running fingers through his hair, he cursed looking out over the horizon. "Give me the fucking gun," he said, holding his hand out. Judi handed him the gun. The sun had set and wouldn't be making an appearance for a good few hours. "Get your clothes off," he said, removing his jacket. Ripper turned his back giving her privacy.

"I'm so sorry, Ripper," she said.

"I don't want to hear it. You're going to do as you're fucking told without comment." He held his jacket out for her to take. "Get on my bike."

She straddled his bike, holding on to him. He drove to one of the exclusive hotels designed for special clients needing an hour a time room. Ripper waited for the key then helped Judi up to the top floor, letting her into the hotel room. "Don't let anyone in. Take a shower and get the shit off you. I'll shout your name when I get back. Don't answer the door to anyone else." He didn't stay behind to hold her hand or console her. The last thing he needed was to waste time. *What the fuck were you doing out this late at night alone, Princess?*

Slamming the door closed he headed back to his bike and the scene of the crime. Before leaving he turned the inner light off, shutting off the ignition. No one had passed when he returned. Thinking about the bullet, Ripper knew he couldn't let the guy he was about to call see the gunshot wound. Grabbing the door, he slammed the car door onto the fucker's face. Each movement stopped the man from looking like anything. The gun was still pressed to his back, reminding him what a fucking asshole he'd been to give it to her. Once he finished he looked at the mess in front of him, and then he called Curse. The other biker would help without too many questions. There would be questions but the other man wouldn't demand an answer.

Pulling out his cell phone, he dialed Curse's number.

"This better be fucking good," Curse said, answering on the third ring.

"I need you, brother."

"I've got a tight pussy on my cock and another waiting for my attention. Can't it wait?"

"It's a cleanup. No one else is as good as you."

He heard the cursing over the line.

"You fucking owe me."

The line went dead. Ripper smiled imagining the women mourning Curse's loss. Before Lexie tamed Devil, their leader had been the man with all the pussy. Now, it was up to Curse to keep them all satisfied. Ripper smiled thinking about Lexie. She was a sweet woman and a fucking hot bitch. He'd heard her screams as Devil fucked her hard. Devil never took her in front of them like he used to other women. Their leader was possessive of his wife, and Ripper understood why. She was a keeper.

Staring at the mess, he waited for Curse to arrive. He blanked all thought of Lexie out of his mind. She didn't deserve to be part of this mess. Neither did Judi. The young girl—woman—had been through more than her fair share of pain. Fuck, he, along with all of his other brothers, had promised along with all of his other brothers to protect her. The sound of the truck approaching alerted Ripper to someone else's presence.

He spotted Curse coming out looking ready to cause trouble. "I had a fucking tight cunt wrapped around my dick. What couldn't wait 'til the morning?"

Ripper pointed at the car. "We need to get this shit cleared away."

"What the fuck happened here?" Curse asked, folding his arms.

Staying silent, Ripper glared at the other man.

"You pulled me away from pussy and you're not even going to give me a good reason as to why?"

They were both immovable.

The battle kept on going for several minutes. Neither of them was moving, and Ripper thought about Judi. Shit, he couldn't leave her alone for too long.

"I owe you. When you need me and can't go to another brother, I'll do whatever you need. Please, for fuck's sake, help me."

"This has gotten a woman written all over it. You're not fucking up the code of dicking a minor, are you?"

"Fuck no." Ripper moved to the truck, sliding open the side door to see the cleaning equipment. "We need to dispose of the body. Don't give a fuck who he is, but he can't be found with the car."

"You want to pretend he left the car to burn?"

Curse asked.

"Yeah. Whatever keeps the two separate."

"This woman must be really fucking special."

Ripper didn't know why he didn't speak the truth to Curse, seeing as the other man would keep it to himself, but then he thought about Judi. She'd called him, no one else. She clearly didn't want any of the others to know what had gone down, but he hated keeping the secrets. This was not for him to tell but for Judi when she was ready.

"This is not how I envisioned the night after the barbeque. Did you see some of The Skulls? They looked so fucking happy." Curse kept talking as they worked, moving the body onto a bag to wrap up.

"I saw."

"Are you still hung up on Lexie?" Curse asked.

"No." He wasn't hung up on her. She was a woman he wanted to wet his dick in, nothing more. Lexie was his president's woman and out of bounds to him.

"Don't worry. Tiny and his crew headed home. It was fun seeing them. They were shit scared we were going to cause a fuss." Curse laughed.

Ripper recalled the time they visited Fort Wills and the deal Devil had to make for them all to be good.

For the next couple of hours, they cleaned all the mess then set fire to the car to leave it.

"Cops here always leave these kinds of investigations alone. Burned out car, no sign of anyone coming and going," Curse said. "There will be nothing leading this shit back to us. They won't find a body and won't go looking either."

"He's not going to be found any time soon. Do you want a lift back to the club?"

"No, I've got shit I got to do." Ripper pulled his bike out of the back of the truck. "No one needs to know about this shit, promise me?"

"I promise. God, I'm not some fucking pussy." Curse left him, heading down the street and out of sight. Straddling his bike, Ripper went to the hotel, knocking on the door and calling out. He stood waiting, looking over his shoulder to see the rising sun.

****

Judi dried her hair coming out of the bathroom after her third shower. Her skin was red raw from all the scrubbing she'd been doing. Every time she looked down she saw the blood over her flesh. She couldn't stop the whimper that escaped her lips nor the panic at the sight. Each shower she scrubbed her skin trying to get the blood and wipe away the memories of what she had done.

Hearing the knock followed by Ripper's call had her running to the door. She didn't know why she'd called him instead of Devil, except that her adoptive father would have gotten Lexie involved, and she didn't the other woman to see her differently.

In the last couple of years she'd grown close to Ripper. He was a sweet man even if he was scary as hell to look at. She doubted he ever smiled. Judi couldn't remember a time when she saw him smile. He listened, talking to her, but never giving anything of himself away.

She felt safe around him. Judi also knew he'd had a bit of a thing for Lexie, which she would never bring up. Lexie was a beautiful woman, even heavily pregnant. All of the crew adored her, but then she was Devil's wife. They didn't really have a choice.

Ripper stepped into the room, closing and locking the door behind him. She saw the state of his clothing.

"The shower is free."

He didn't say anything, brushing past her to go to the bathroom. She couldn't stop looking at his red hair.

Never in her life had she found a red-haired man all that attractive, but with Ripper it worked. It didn't stand out all that much. She couldn't even believe she was thinking about his hair at a time like this. Ripper was not the kind of man she went for. He was one of Devil's close friends, including hers. Closing her eyes, she settled on the edge of the bed waiting for him to appear. She wore a robe that she'd found in the hotel.

Ten minutes later, Ripper appeared with a towel wrapped around his waist. He placed the gun onto the bed beside her.

"What the fuck were you doing outside without protection?" he asked, glaring down at her.

She took in his hard muscles. There was a six pack that looked rock hard decorating his abs. Judi knew he worked out. She'd seen him working many times but not given his body much thought. Ink decorated his sides, and she saw the name "Chaos" on one side while on the other "Bleeds" decorated his body in fancy writing. Other tattoos were of snakes, tribal tattoos, and many more.

Each piece of ink was a testament to his time with the crew. The crew went everywhere together. It was only Vincent who settled down to stay with his wife in town.

"You better fucking answer me, Judi. I'm not in the fucking mood to deal with your silent treatment."

"I wanted to go out for a walk, okay?" She looked up at him, glaring.

"What?"

"I was sick and tired of listening to all of them being so fucking happy." She stood up putting her hands on her hips. "I can never have that, and I went out for a walk. I didn't even think. I only wanted to be away from it all. Away from college, away from being a fucking princess, away from it all." Judi felt like such a bitch for letting her anger get the better of her. This man had taken care of her mess, and all she'd done was shout at him, which he didn't deserve. "Sorry—"

He held his hand up in front of her face stopping her. "No, you've had your fucking say." Ripper gripped her arms, turning her to press against the wall. His hand landed around her neck, and he stared into her eyes.

For the first time since knowing the man in front of her, she was afraid.

"Let's get one thing straight, Judi. I don't give a fuck who you are. I could kill you right now, and Devil wouldn't be any the fucking wiser." He tightened his fingers around her neck, showing his true threat. "People who spoke to me the way you just did end up fucking dead." He loosened his hold but didn't drop his hands from around her neck. "I dealt with your fucking mess, but it will never leave this room. Neither of us will ever talk about it again, do you understand?"

"Yes," she said, nodding, frightened of him.

"You were a prostitute, Judi. I don't hold it against you. Shit, you shouldn't have gone through that kind of shit at all. It's behind you, but you took on the club, and you will live by the club rules."

He let her go, and his eyes were once again bland where seconds ago they'd been terrifyingly cold. She placed a hand to her neck, wondering what he was going to do. He watched the action but didn't offer her an apology.

"If you hate me so much why do you put up with me?" she asked, watching him sit on the edge of the bed. Judi inwardly cringed at her behavior. Since Chaos Bleeds had taken her away from the hell of her life, she'd been pampered with the princess role they gave her. She had to stop being a spoiled brat. Ripper had helped her tonight, and she needed to remember that.

"I don't hate you, Judi. Regardless of what I just said I wouldn't kill you because I happen to like and care about you." He looked up at her.

His muscles stood out, and for the first time in her life she felt the pulse between her thighs. "I care about you, too."

"When Devil asks, you tell him you spent some time with a girlfriend."

"I don't have a girlfriend." She didn't have any friends.

"Make up an excuse for him to be satisfied." He picked up the gun. "You're not getting this back. I don't trust you not to fuck up big time."

"I messed up," she said, agreeing. She hated him being mad at her, and after the way she'd spoken to him, he had every right to be.

"It's a good job you know that." He let out a sigh looking around the room. "This is not how I expected to spend the night." There was only one double bed.

Judi watched him stand up, going to the top of the bed and pulling down the blankets.

"I'm not sleeping on the floor. You better be okay sharing this bed with me."

"I've never shared a bed with a man before." She stopped, feeling her cheeks heat. There were a lot of things she hadn't done with a man or boy.

"Come on then, Princess, in you get." He slid inside settling onto the pillow. She kept the robe on thinking about what she hadn't done. She'd never been on a date or been kissed by a boy that she actually wanted to be kissed by. There was never a time to go parking in the car and get felt up. Tears filled her eyes as she remembered what she had done because of her pimp, Rob. He'd taken her, and before she knew what happened, men were taking pleasure out of her.

Rob's treatment had been a weekend of being available for the men. Every hole had a use, he would taunt. Her stomach rolled at the acrid memories. Running to the bathroom she bent over the toilet seat letting out everything she'd eaten that night.

Seconds later she felt Ripper rubbing her hair, holding it out of her way. She heaved, spilling the contents down the pan. Over and over she threw up.

"I've got you, baby. Keep it coming." His voice soothed her.

She saw the man with a hole in his head. He'd talked about that weekend of her being broken in, and she'd lost it. That one memory was something she wanted rid of.

Sinking down to the floor, she cried wishing she didn't know the evil of some men. Ripper was a man capable of doing evil things, but he wasn't into forcing a woman. His arms surrounded her along with his heat.

"I've got you."

He picked her up, and she was surprised by how easily he carried her to the bed. In the last two years she'd put on a little bit of weight, filling out into a size fourteen figure. Okay, most of her clothes were getting toward a size sixteen, but she refused to believe it. Lexie's cooking was amazing, and she could never turn it down.

"Memories are the things we can't fight, Princess. You're going to have to learn to accept them and move on."

"It was horrible," she said.

"I know, but that fucker is dead and not coming back."

"How many men have you killed?" she asked.

"I'm not going to answer that."

"Have you killed women?" The question slipped past her lips.

"I'm not answering that either." He kissed her temple. "Go to sleep. I'll hold you when the nightmares come."

She closed her eyes, and Ripper wasn't lying. He held her throughout each nightmare. Every time he smoothed her back, and she was able to think once again.

Chapter Two

Opening his eyes, Ripper became aware of the full woman lying in his arms. He stared at the long length of brown hair covering his arms then down at the face. His cock was rock fucking hard. Seeing Judi's sweet face had him jumping out of bed. She squealed, but he was heading toward the bathroom before she caught sight of his morning boner. *Fuck, shit, fuck, shit.* There was no excuse for him to be getting a fucking hard-on.

Dealing with his morning routine, he waited for his body to get back under control before heading out. He caught sight of his clothes and cursed. Last night he'd been so determined to get back to the hotel that he'd forgotten to grab some clothes for Judi.

Quickly putting his clothes on, he opened the door. He found Judi standing outside the door with her legs crossed. Moving out of the way he waited for her to shut the door.

"I'm going to get you some clothes," he said.

"Okay." Her voice was a whisper.

Ignoring the yearning in his soul, he left the room, getting on his bike and heading to the nearest store. He parked in the parking lot, entering the cheap department store and grabbing clothes from the racks. With his arms wrapped around her, Ripper had a good idea of her measurements. She'd put some meat on her bones living with Lexie. He didn't mind. Years of fucking bags of bones had made him appreciate a woman with curves every day of the week, and Lexie had made him appreciate a woman with curves even more. He'd seen her dancing, and that was a fucking orgasm waiting to happen.

Paying for the jeans, shirt, and plain as shit underwear, he headed back to the hotel. He let himself inside, finding her on the edge of the bed with her fingers locked together. Handing the bag to her, he took a seat, picking up the remote.

"Get dressed and I'll drop you off home."

"Ripper?"

"We're not talking about shit. Remember, nothing happened?"

She nodded, not saying anything, disappearing into the bathroom. He wasn't looking at her shapely legs either. Turning back to the television he cursed his fucking weakness.

He needed to fuck a woman, and the sooner he did it the better. Watching some design program on television he waited for Judi to come out. Minutes passed, and she finally came out. Her brown hair was bound on top of her head. When he first saw her, her hair had been short. In the last couple of years she'd grown out the silky curls. He wondered what they would feel like as he ran his fingers through the strands.

Get a woman, fuck her, and stop thinking this shit.

Turning the television off, he got to his feet and headed toward the door. "Are you coming?" He picked up his jacket waiting for her to follow.

Locking the door, he took the key back to the main reception. Judi was waiting beside his bike.

He climbed on waiting for her to straddle the back of his bike. Feeling her arms surround him had his cock jerking in response. He was not fucking doing this. Gunning his machine, he headed toward the street ready to drop her off.

Breaking the speed limit, he got to her street. She climbed off, handing him back the helmet. He took it without meeting her eyes. There was no way he was going to let this shit happen to him. Judi was the club princess. She was off limits to the likes of him.

Ripper watched Judi walk up to the house she shared with Devil and Lexie. He made sure she was inside before he turned back heading toward the clubhouse.

Entering the clubhouse he saw the mess straight away. Devil was going to fucking lose it. Going to the bar, he grabbed a bottle of whiskey and then grabbed one of the first women he came across. She had black hair, pale skin, and was more than willing to fuck anything.

"Hey, Ripper. I missed you," she said.

"What's your name again?" he asked.

"Ashley." She giggled, wrapping her arms around his neck. He picked her up, carrying her toward the room he kept inside the clubhouse. They all had their own space, and no one invaded others' rooms. He kicked the door closed, dropping Ashley to the bed. Taking a long gulp from the whiskey bottle, he watched her unbutton his jeans. She took out his cock, which wasn't even hard.

She took him into his mouth, and he moaned, sinking his fingers in her dark hair. Ashley had been hanging around the club for the past year. Most of the men, apart from Vincent and Devil, had fucked her. She loved cock and couldn't get enough of all of them. He imagined she also loved the lifestyle of not having to work providing she gave them pussy whenever they demanded. He didn't have a problem with taking her pussy when the need demanded.

Waking up beside Judi with a hard-on wasn't an experience he wanted to repeat. The one woman he didn't want to be having a hard-on for was Judi. She meant too much to the club to risk losing his life over. Ashley moaned pulling his mind away from the other woman he'd spent the night with.

Being with Judi would fuck him up. Devil would

never allow him to live. She had the club protection, which meant she was untouchable. Feeling sick to his stomach, he sank his fingers into Ashley's hair, forcing her to take more of his dick.

"Fuck, suck it good."

When she got him nice and hard, he grabbed a condom, quickly protected himself and slammed deep into her hot little pussy. They both moaned, and her pussy worked his dick like they were born to be together. Staying still within her, he took another long swill of whiskey.

"Who are you trying to forget?" Ashley asked.

He slapped her ass, shutting her up. Putting the bottle on the floor, he gripped her hips and plunged into her pussy, pounding away inside her. She didn't complain once about the depth or thickness of his dick. Ripper wouldn't have stopped. He needed to orgasm or he wasn't going to be able to get over what happened this morning.

Closing his eyes, he fucked Ashley hard, using her to find his own release. She was already taking care of her own orgasm, stroking her clit until she went over the edge. He dropped her hips, leaving her to fall to the bed. Removing the condom and throwing it in the trash, he grabbed her head and got her to lick his cock clean of his cum. Ripper watched her tongue licking up every white droplet of his cream.

"That's it, baby. Take it all." He started to get hard once again watching her lick him. "Do you want a load in your throat?" he asked, knowing he wasn't going to stop until he came again.

Ashley spent the next twenty minutes sucking on his cock until he came, giving her a wad of his cum. He watched her swallow him down. Only when he was satisfied did he let her go.

"Fuck me, Ripper. You're a fucking dirty bastard. You really do love fucking, don't you?" she asked, wiping a hand across her forehead.

Taking a long gulp of whiskey he tried not to think of the guilt at what he'd just done. An image of Judi's sleeping face entered his mind, and the guilt made him feel like throwing up at what he'd just done.

"Get out," he said, swigging down more whiskey.

He saw the spark of hurt in her eyes but didn't care. When his door closed, he collapsed to the bed feeling the exhaustion of everything he'd done. Minutes later Curse appeared, leaning against the doorframe with arms folded.

"What?" Ripper asked.

"You come in from being out all night, fuck Ashley, and upset her. I hate to say this, but she's one of the good ones, Ripper." Curse rarely spoke up for any woman let alone a club sweet-butt.

"What the fuck do you want?"

"I need breakfast, and you need to apologize to Ashley. She did nothing wrong last night."

Staring at his ceiling, Ripper pictured Judi.

"I'm not hungry."

"Get fucking hungry. I helped you out last night. You owe me, and it's going to take too fucking long for me to allow you to live it down." Curse hadn't moved from the doorway, but his disapproval was felt deep into the room.

"She's a club whore. Ashley means nothing."

Glancing at Curse, he knew it was the wrong thing to say. "There are many men downstairs who would disagree. She's a nice woman and wouldn't hurt this club for anything. Ashley is not jealous of anyone, and she has a good friendship with Lexie and with Phoebe. She doesn't go near the men who are taken and respects everyone."

"Fine, I'm going for a shower, and then I'll come to fucking breakfast."

Getting to his feet, he headed for the shower, washing the morning off.

****

Judi let herself into the kitchen. She walked into the house around the back way not expecting anyone to be up yet.

"Where the fuck have you been?" Devil asked.

She spun around finding him sitting at the counter with Elizabeth in her high chair. He was feeding her breakfast and was dressed in a pair of sweat pants. Judi knew it had taken him some time getting used to wearing clothes around the house while she was home. The first time they'd come face to face with his dick hanging out would haunt her forever.

"Erm, I was at a friend's," she said, thinking about Ripper's excuse.

"You don't have any friends." He gave another spoonful of food to Elizabeth then turned his gaze back to her.

"I've got friends."

"No, you haven't. I've heard you telling Lexie enough times."

"Lexie and I were alone during those conversations." Had Lexie told him her complaints? She hoped not. Judi would never trust the other woman again.

"Regardless of what you think, Lexie would never break your trust. She's rarely alone, and I keep an eye on her constantly." He pointed in the corner of the kitchen. She glanced back to see a small camera.

"You're spying on her?"

"Not spying. I'm taking care of what's mine. Lexie is my woman. She belongs to me and the club. If I can't always be here then I will keep an eye on her at all times." Devil didn't even look remorseful.

"You should be ashamed of yourself," she said, hating how much he would know about her. Who else knew about the cameras?

"My woman, my rules. I will never let any harm come to her. Also, any boy you think of bringing here will be seen as well."

"You're insane." She folded her arms over her chest wishing she could say something to him to stop him from invading Lexie's privacy.

"Will you two stop fighting?" Lexie said, rounding the corner. Her hair was piled on top of her head, much like Judi's. She wore a vest style shirt and a pair of sweat pants showing off her rounded stomach. Devil pretty much kept her pregnant.

"I was giving you time to sleep," Devil said, getting up to wrap his arms around her.

"I know. It's hard to sleep when Simon likes throwing his playing bricks against the wall." She wiped the sleep from her eyes. Judi was concerned for her friend. She looked really poorly this morning.

"Are you all right?" Judi asked.

"Yeah, I'll be fine." Lexie pressed a hand to her mouth then her stomach, going pale. "I swear I'm going to be sick twenty-four hours."

Judi took over feeding Elizabeth as Devil went to deal with Simon. There were many bad things she could say about Devil, but she saw the love he had for Lexie. Many nights she would watch the couple. Devil spent most of his time watching Lexie doing something or other.

"What's going on between you two?" Lexie asked, sitting down and nibbling on some crackers.

"Nothing. He's being overbearing and an ass."

She finished feeding Elizabeth then stood. "I'm going to grab a shower."

"What are you doing today?"

"I'm going to head to the library," Judi said, needing to get out of the house. If Devil was watching their every movement then she needed to get out of the way.

"Okay, I'm going to Phoebe's with the kids. We're having a girly day."

Judi kissed her friend's cheek then headed upstairs. She closed the door to her bedroom, and then she kept her back to the door and slid to the floor. Covering her face, Judi wondered what she was going to do with the rest of her life. At one stage she was going to be a social worker but soon decided it was not something she wanted to do with her life. Then she thought about caring for others in their home. She closed her eyes, wondering what she was going to do. Devil was providing a lot of money for her education.

Being a nurse was out of the question as she hated the sight of blood.

You killed a man last night.

Cutting the thoughts off, she climbed to her feet heading toward the shower. The clothes Ripper had bought her were a perfect fit. He knew her size, and she didn't know if she should be embarrassed with him knowing the real size.

Tugging the band from her hair, she left the waves to fall down around her face. When Rob got his claws inside her and started to hurt her every time one of the clients complained, he took to pulling her around by her hair. She hated it, and when he wasn't forcing her to fuck, she hacked away at the length with some blunt scissors.

In the last two years her hair had grown full and

long. She stared at the length remembering the man last night, gripping the strands.

"You're a fucking whore. The only thing you're good for is sucking cock, riding cock. Women like you need it in your mouth, cunt, and ass."

She pulled out of her memory with a gasp. His comments had ended with him getting a bullet in his head. Splashing cold water onto her face, she turned the shower on and made sure the water was freezing.

Cold to the bone, she climbed out, grabbed a towel and entered her bedroom. She searched through her wardrobe settling on a pair of jeans and a red shirt. Toeing some flip-flops onto her feet, she grabbed her bag and headed downstairs.

Devil was kissing Lexie at the doorway, stroking her sides.

"I'm fine."

"You'll text me, ring me if anything is different," Devil asked.

"Of course. Stop panicking. Phoebe will be taking good care of me. You know how protective she gets." Lexie smiled at him.

He wrapped his arms around her shoulders then stared at her. "Are you going to town?" he asked.

She nodded, putting the bag on her shoulders. "Yes, will you give me a lift?"

"Sure."

Smiling toward Lexie, Judi climbed on the back of Devil's bike, giving her friend a wave. She held onto Devil's waist as he headed into town. He pulled up outside of the library, waiting for her to climb off. "What's wrong with Lexie?" Judi asked, concerned.

"She's struggling with this pregnancy. Her sickness is bad. The doctors are keeping an eye on her."

"I take it if anything happens to her, the doctors

won't make it to nightfall." Judi was joking, but she saw the seriousness on Devil's face.

"You're my daughter in the eyes of the law, Judi. I adopted you, and when I do that, you're my family. Lexie is the woman who owns my heart and soul. If anything happens to her, I will kill anyone who could have stopped it."

Judi swallowed past the lump in her throat. It was sweet, if not a little scary. "I'm sure she'll be fine."

"She better be otherwise Piston County will have three dead doctors." Devil left her alone with his parting words.

Yes, she hoped nothing was wrong with Lexie other than the early stages of pregnancy.

Walking into the library, she signed into the computer using her details. She wasn't at college at the moment as it was a break, but she still had assignments she had to finish. Her education was something she was proud of. After everything she'd been through, she'd passed her exams with a good grade. She had several papers she needed to write. Once she signed in, leaving her bag beside the computer, she grabbed a couple of books and started to work through her paper.

The moment she started studying all thought of what happened last night went out of her mind. Nothing and no one could hurt her here. The only thought she couldn't get out of her mind was Ripper and his naked body so close to her face. He'd grabbed her around the neck, threatening her, but she felt sick as she wasn't even scared of him.

Get over it, Judi. It's never going to happen.

Resting her head in her hand she read through the many articles in the book, typing away at the computer. She could have done all this work at home, but she would have been distracted too easily. Working in the computer room, helped to put her troubled thoughts at ease.

Keep working.

I wonder what his lips would feel like.

The thought had her gasping and closing the book she was reading. The sound of the book closing drew several gazes. Getting up from her seat she placed the book back on the shelf. Thinking about Ripper's lips was not something she could do.

Looking across at the diner, her stomach started to rumble. She needed food. With food she would stop having these stupid thoughts about Ripper. Shutting down the computer and hiking her bag on her shoulder, she headed out of the library.

Chapter Three

Ripper sat opposite Ashley and Curse. There was a group of them waiting to be served breakfast. Pussy, Death, and Spider were also sat around the closest booths with several of the clubs sweet-butts. He saw the waitresses made a wide berth of them refusing to come and take their orders.

"We're not going to get served," Ripper said, looking over the menu. There were several meals he wanted to try.

"Mia will be here soon. She'll serve us," Ashley said, looking down at the menu.

"Who is Mia?" Curse asked.

"She's my friend."

"Why haven't we seen her at the club?" Pussy asked.

From the look of some of the women, they really didn't like Ashley all that much. Ripper saw all the men liked Ashley. He wondered what she'd done for them to give her the respect usually reserved for an old lady.

"Mia's not one for the partying or the clubs. She was at college until six months ago when her mother got sick. Her waste of a space father cut and ran with his secretary, and she's been surviving ever since." Ashley kept talking, and they all paid attention, apart from the women. She looked up, glancing around the diner. "Here she comes now."

Ripper looked in the direction where she was. A woman with similar black hair was approaching their table. She wore the waitressing uniform, and it didn't hide her curves. Fuck, this woman knew how to walk. Glancing at Curse, he saw his friend hadn't taken his eyes off her.

"Hey, Ash, sorry I'm late." Mia was patting her

pockets and searching for the pencil to take down their orders. She looked frazzled in a charming kind of way. Ripper expected her to take one look at them and leave. The leather along with the design on their cuts scared a lot of women away.

"What's up?" Ashley asked.

"Nothing. I had to run to the pharmacy to grab Mom's prescription. Almost didn't make it back for my shift." She glanced behind her at the other women. "No one else will serve you?"

"Nah, they're scared."

Mia nodded. "Okay, what can I get you all?"

Ashley made her order first, and the men waited to see if Mia walked away. After a few seconds, Mia looked up. "Are you the only one eating?" Her gaze went to all the men.

They all joined in, ordering their breakfast. Ripper watched Curse, who hadn't taken his eyes off Mia. Once she finished writing she left them to it.

It was strange not to be judged by their cut. He was so used to having some women scamper away from them while others were all over him like a rash. Mia didn't look scared of them. If anything, she looked more annoyed at the lack of women offering to take their orders.

"She seems nice," Curse said.

"Mia's a sweetie-pie. I just wish she knew how to relax."

"Doesn't she judge you from hanging out with us?" Pussy asked, speaking up.

"Nope. I told her how happy I was, and she didn't have a complaint to say." Ashley looked held her cup out as Mia returned to pour them all a drink. Curse was quiet throughout it all.

Ripper knew why but kept his smile to himself.

His friend had always loved a quiet, dark haired beauty.

The door to the diner opened, and his own torment entered. Judi hadn't even seen them in the diner. "Look who it is," Curse said, nodding toward her.

His voice gained her attention, and she looked toward them. Ripper recognized the fake smile. She was not expecting to see them inside.

"Hey, guys, you here for breakfast?" she asked, approaching the table.

"I think it's more lunchtime now," Ashley said, smiling. "Do you want to sit with us?"

"No, I've got some reading to do." She nodded at each of them avoiding his eyes. He tried not to watch her head to the back of the diner. Mia returned carrying their food.

Ripper watched as Curse leaned in to smell her skin. The movement was slight, but their friendship was long. He recognized movements that others didn't.

Mia left them alone to deal with Judi.

"I see someone has gained your attention," Ripper said.

Curse glared at him while Ashley perked up. "Really, who?"

"Nothing." Both men answered together. Biting into his pancakes, Ripper tried to ignore the woman in the back of the diner. When everyone finished, Ashley said goodbye to her friend. He stayed behind so he could have a word with Judi. She looked too pale for his liking, and he hated to think about her suffering.

Looking out of the window, he saw the last of the bikes disappearing before heading to the back and sitting opposite the woman who was plaguing his thoughts.

She tensed as he sat down.

"What's the matter?" she asked.

"Nothing, I wanted to see how you were doing."

He leaned back, watching her.

Judi paused, putting her fork down onto her plate. "I'm fine, Ripper."

Staring into her dark brown eyes, he wondered what was going on in that head of hers. She had always fascinated him, but he'd cut any of the thoughts or curiosity from his mind. For the first time in the last two years, he wanted to get to know more.

"Really?"

"What did you want me to say?" She hadn't picked up her fork to eat some more.

Leaning over, he snagged one of her pancakes and ate it himself. "Last night you killed a man. I'm not a fucking idiot, and I don't need a degree to know it fucks with people's heads." His first kill had left him reeling for days. To get over it he'd drunk, done drugs, and fucked every pussy available to him to stop thinking about what he'd done. Being in the club helped him even more.

Tears filled her eyes, and she looked down at her food.

"I'm trying not to think about it."

Her voice was only a whisper, but he caught the sadness in her tone.

"You need to think about it but get over it."

She looked up, glaring at him. "You told me not to mention it outside of that hotel room. Why are you forcing me to talk about it?"

"Because I was being an ass, and you deserve better. Killing a man doesn't make things easier. I took care of it, but you need to take care of it here." He pressed his fingers to her temple.

"I'm never going to be able to get over it. I killed a man."

"I know. I've killed many."

She closed her eyes, picking up her fork to start playing with her food. "How did you handle it?"

"The usual way, drinking, snorting, and fucking. I doubt it's going to work that way for you."

Judi shook her head. "I've fucked enough men."

His hands fisted at his sides. "Don't," he said.

"Don't what? It's the truth."

"No, it's not. You were fucked by men, forced to do it. You were never willing."

"How do you know?" she asked, glaring at him.

"A willing woman doesn't get beaten black and blue by their pimp."

Her cheeks were bright red. Reaching over, he took hold of her hand. "I bet you don't even know what it's like to experience a real orgasm."

Shut up, Ripper.

He didn't listen to reason. "Do you even know what it's like to have a man filled with the need to pleasure you, licking your sweet pussy?"

She gasped, looking up at him. "Ripper, what are you doing?"

"Nothing. Fucking nothing." He stood up, throwing some notes down onto the counter. "If you ever need me, call me."

He stormed out of the diner, straddling his bike. What the fuck was his problem? Judi was not his problem to deal with. She was twenty years old and deserved a life of love and happiness, where all her dreams come true. He wasn't the kind of man to give such a commitment.

Pulling out of the town, he felt the wind on his face, not caring he wasn't wearing a helmet. Safety was for fucking pussies.

Ripper drove for the next couple of hours, his thoughts tormented by Judi. She shouldn't be invading his thoughts or even occasioning his sexual ones. When he got back to the club he found Devil and Lexie hanging out. Vincent and Phoebe were absent along with the kids.

Lexie was curled up against Devil looking pale. She was rubbing her stomach and sipping some water. Her head rested on Devil's knee. Nodding his head toward his president, Ripper went to his room to focus on his feelings for Judi. She was just a woman and one he couldn't fuck.

Never going to have Judi. Stop thinking about her. She's not yours.

Lying back against his bed, Ripper growled as her face entered his thoughts. What the fuck was he going to do?

****

What the hell just happened?

Judi stared at the empty seat opposite her completely baffled by what happened. Picking up her fork she took a bite of her pancake then another. His words had made her wet between her thighs. Finishing off her food, she headed back to the library to finish off her computer work. By the time five o'clock came she was exhausted and headed back home. The walk was a long one, and she entered home an hour later. Lexie was in the kitchen stirring some kind of sauce on the stove.

"Hey," Judi said.

"Hey, Devil and the kids are at the dinner table if you want to join them."

"Should you be working?"

"I'm fine, honey. It's just the start, and I'll get over it. Women have been giving birth for centuries."

They've also been dying because of it.

Judi kept her thoughts to herself and entered the sitting room. Elizabeth was playing with a book while Simon was pressing buttons on his toy making noise. She saw Devil bowed over a book reading.

"Anything interesting?" Judi asked.

He lifted the book up, and she saw it was a pregnancy bible.

"Still worried about her sickness?"

"Yes, she wasn't like this with Elizabeth, and I'm not risking shit because of it."

Nodding, she put her bag down, grabbing another pregnancy book from the shelf in the corner of the room. Twenty minutes later Lexie walked in, hissing as she saw what they were doing. "Stop it, you two. I'm perfectly fine. Now stop trying to fix something that's not there." She set their plates in front of them.

"Baby, I'm going to keep looking until I find out what's wrong with you."

No one, not even Lexie, was going to tell Devil what to do and not to do. Lexie sighed but didn't actually argue with him.

"Fine, don't worry though. It's morning sickness and nothing else." Lexie sat down and dived into her food.

Judi ate with relish loving the spicy sauce. She noticed Devil's gaze was constantly on Lexie, and yearning hit her hard.

What would it be like to have a man who loved her as much as Devil loved Lexie? After dinner she did the dishes making sure Lexie rested. Wiping down the work surfaces, she thought about Ripper and his comment. She'd never experienced a single orgasm or known what true passion was all about. Closing her bedroom door she rested her head against the wood wishing Ripper hadn't said anything earlier at the diner. Her thoughts were constantly on sex and nothing else. She'd been with so many men, and yet faced with Ripper's raw sexuality she didn't know how she was going to cope. Her emotions were completely fried. Life was better when she didn't have to think about sex or men or anything but her coursework.

Moving away from the door, she went to the bathroom and started her nighttime routine. It was only seven, but she needed to wash the day's sweat and grime from her body. Even sitting in the library had caused her to sweat in the heat. There was no air conditioning inside the small building. Standing underneath the shower she let the hot water scald her body.

Thoughts of Ripper's large capable hands holding her invaded her mind. Pressing her palms to the tiles she bit her lip trying to contain the whimper of need threatening to escape.

You don't deserve love or lust.
You're a whore and a killer.

Turning the heat to cold she gasped at the sudden lashing of ice attacking her skin. When she couldn't take the chill she turned the water off, climbing out. She wrapped a towel around her body and then around her hair. The mirror was steamed, and when she wiped her hand across to view she gasped as the man from last night stared back at her. Closing her eyes, heart pounding, she forced herself to look back in the mirror to find herself staring right back at her.

"He's gone, and he's not coming back."

Entering her bedroom she heard her cell phone beep. Frowning, she went to see who it was.

Ripper: What you doing?

What the hell was going on with him? They'd gotten along well for the last couple of years, but he never checked up on her.

Judi: I'm home if that's what you're worried about.

Throwing the cell to the bed she quickly dried her

hair before running a brush through the length. She loved taking the time to get rid of every knot. When she first moved in with Devil, she would spend hours brushing her hair. Lexie would take over when her arms ached. The cell phone buzzed again. Dropping the brush to the bed she picked up the small device.

Ripper: Want to go somewhere?
Judi: Don't you have a club whore to fuck?
Ripper: No! Want to go for a ride?

Glancing at the door, Judi wondered what the hell he was doing. Ripper was her friend, yet he kept a good distance from her.

Ripper: Well?

Devil and Lexie never checked on her anymore. There was one time Devil had walked in while she was getting dressed. She'd screamed at him, and he'd turned bright red and left. Since then, neither of them entered the room.

Judi: Pick me up in ten.
Ripper: Rebel!

She smiled, going to her wardrobe and putting on a pair of jeans followed by a shirt. Tying her hair up in a ponytail she went toward her window. Slowly she climbed down from her bedroom using the brackets for Lexie's hanging baskets for support. Lexie was standing in the kitchen, and she heard Devil talking.

"I don't want anything to happen to you," Devil said, wrapping his arms around her waist.

"I'm sure there'll be plenty of pussy to replace me."

Judi watched as Devil caught hold of Lexie's chin, turning her to face him. "I don't give a fuck about any other pussy but yours. Promise me if this starts to feel like more you'll tell me."

The raw emotion on his face cut Judi deeply. This

was the kind of love people wrote about, but they tamed it to make it readable. Devil would die for Lexie and vice versa. Walking away, she left the couple to their moment. Ripper was waiting for her down the road with his main light turned off.

"Come on, Princess. Let's go and have some fun." He handed her a helmet waiting for her to climb on the back of his bike.

"What's gotten into you?" she asked.

"I don't know. I needed a ride and wanted your company."

She held onto his waist as he gunned the machine. Pressing her head against his back she felt the power between her thighs as his bike rode the road. Ripper was an expert, and each turn had her tightening her grip.

"I'm not going to put you at risk. Stop panicking." He shouted to be heard over the wind and noise.

Closing her eyes, Judi basked in the freedom. Rob had taken away her freedom trapping her in cars, hotel rooms or even her apartment with men she didn't want near her. She had been with them all, fat, thin, businessmen, thugs, even guys she used to go to school with. Judi shivered forcing her eyes tightly closed to rid the memories from her thoughts. She was no longer the town whore, along with all Rob's other women.

Devil had taken her away from the pain and the stench of sex. Would she ever know what it felt like to be made love to?

The time passed with Ripper working the roads until he pulled up outside a late night diner. They entered taking a seat at the back.

"What are we doing here?" she asked, sitting opposite him.

"I'm hungry and thirsty. Order what you want. Food is on me."

She glanced down the menu as the waitress took his order of three hamburgers and fries with all the trimmings including slaw. Judi took a milkshake and a burger.

"Wow, how do you not weigh over a ton?" she asked.

"I work the shit off every day."

"Yeah, I heard fucking was a good weight loss program." Judi rolled her eyes, chuckling.

Ripper wasn't chuckling. He looked annoyed. "I don't fuck everything that walks."

"I didn't say you did. I don't mind you being a man-whore and all that." She smiled at him, trying to lighten the mood. "Someone has to keep the sweet-butts company."

"Curse is more than enough company for them."

"I'm only joking, Ripper. Out of all of the men the sweet-butts talk about you the least."

He seemed satisfied with her answer. The waitress bought them their food and drinks.

Ripper finished a burger in three bites. Judi stared open mouthed at how much he packed away. He didn't look like a pig at all.

"Does riding do that to you?" she asked.

"How are you handling what happened last night?" He counteracted her question with one of his own.

"Erm, I'm dealing with it, I think."

He stared at her, clearly seeing through her lie.

"I got out of the shower, and I thought I saw him." She stopped to rub at her neck. Her throat felt swollen shut.

"You'll feel that way a long time."

"Did you?"

Chapter Four

Ripper stared at Judi wondering how much he should share with her. His life hadn't always been sunshine and roses. He learned the hard way no one cared about him. Born to a whore, he'd done everything to earn a living. Killing someone had struck him hard the first time, but now, it was second nature. No one messed with him or the brothers of his club. The one salvation in his life was Chaos Bleeds. He owed them everything.

"Yeah, I felt that way. There's no stopping it. We're human, and taking another life still takes its toll." Killing people had long stopped causing him a problem. If someone needed to die, then he was more than happy to do the deed.

"How did you get over it?" she asked.

Glancing over the table he watched her nibble on a burger. She wasn't doing her food any justice. No one nibbled on a burger.

"I couldn't take it back. No matter how much I thought about it, I couldn't bring them back to life. They were dead. I was not. That man you put a bullet in his brain, he would have fucked you that night." He stopped, fisting his hands to try to stop the anger. "That bastard would have forced his dick inside you, Princess. He'd have raped you and probably killed you so you didn't say a thing."

She looked around at the diner. "Why are you saying these things?"

"Because they're true and you need to stop feeling guilty. If it was me, I'd kill him in a heartbeat. You did good to protect yourself."

"I'm surprised you didn't tell Devil. Why haven't you?" she asked. "You don't have to listen to me."

"You want to tell him then do so. I doubt he'd let

you out after dark, and your windows and doors would be nailed fucking shut." He raised a brow waiting for her to see what he was saying. "Devil has taken his daddy role with you. You're his daughter. Don't test him. Otherwise you'll be begging for something different."

He took another bite of his burger waiting for his words to sink in.

"What about you?"

"What about me?" he asked.

Her cheeks went bright red. "Erm, what was all about today at the other diner, talking about sex and orgasms?"

Ripper chuckled. "Wouldn't you like to know?"

There was no denying his attraction to her. He wouldn't take it too far. If he touched her, Devil would kill him. He figured spending time with her would show it wasn't attraction at all but friendship.

"Are you going back to college?" he asked.

"Yeah, I think so. I'm not sure. With Lexie struggling with her recent pregnancy I'm thinking of staying around and doing my work online." She ran fingers through her hair as she spoke.

He'd been counting on her leaving so he could get over this shit that was going on inside him.

"What does Lexie say?"

"She's determined its only morning sickness. Devil's worried. I see the way he looks, and he believes it's something more." She finally took a large bite out of her burger. "Do you want me to leave?" she asked.

"Why do you ask that?"

"I've caused you nothing but trouble. I mean you're only here with me, and I bet you'd have been with a sweet-butt by now or at the strip club."

He shook his head. "No, I'm not here for any other reason than I wanted to spend time with you."

There, he said it.

She stayed silent for the rest of the meal. When they were done he threw down some money then got to his feet.

"Come on, let's get back to town."

Judi put the helmet back on climbing onto the back of his bike. He headed back to Piston County but stopped on one of the highest hills looking over the town. It was a small picnic reserve, and he parked up.

"What are you doing?" she asked, following him. Her hair was a mess, but she looked incredibly cute.

The moon was shining high in the sky overlooking the small town. "Sit with me a little while." He patted the seat beside the bench not wanting their time to end. She took a seat beside him. Her hand lay on the bench between them. Staring at her hand, he returned his gaze back to the view. "I love coming here. We stopped travelling to stay in this town."

"It's so small."

"I know." Unable to stop himself, Ripper covered her hand with his. Compared to his, her hand was so small, tiny even.

He heard her gasp. "What are you thinking?" she asked.

"That there is nowhere I'd rather be than sitting with you looking over where we live. I've been on the road most of my life. I'm not a good man, Judi. In fact, some would say I'm a total fucking bastard, but I can promise you I'd keep you protected and I'll stick to my promise."

"Why are you saying this?"

Ripper didn't respond. He didn't know why he was saying anything. Locking their fingers together he looked out over the view, wishing things were different.

His cock thickened, and he closed his eyes,

wishing it would go away.

"You were right," she said, capturing his attention once again.

"About what?" The sane part of his brain knew where this conversation was going while another just wanted to get it out in the open.

"I've never been kissed before, not by a guy I wanted. You were right about so much."

What the fuck was he going to do?

Devil's going to kill you if you continue.

The image of her lips and her full body against his invaded his thoughts. Since the night before he'd pictured her in many different ways. Even Ashley couldn't replace her beauty. He was fucked.

"Shit, I really shouldn't be doing this." Judi got to her feet about to tug her hand out of his. He held onto her refusing to let go. "This is insane."

Getting to his feet he tugged her close so she had no choice but to fall against him. "I know, but tell me you don't want this and I'll leave you the fuck alone. I'm not a rapist, Princess."

Devil is going to kill you.

Even with the threat running through his mind, he placed a hand on her hip then slid it round to curve over her ass. With Lexie's cooking Judi had filled out in all the right places. Her tits were lovely and full, her ass ripe and her hips rounded.

His cock pulsed harder, pressing against her stomach.

Tilting her head back, he stared into her eyes before dropping his gaze down to her full lips. Her tongue poked out to wet her lips.

"Well, what do you want to do, Judi?" he asked.

Never had he wanted a woman as much as he wanted her.

"I'm not a virgin."

"I'm not asking for a virgin." Ripper wasn't in the mood for fucking women who hadn't known a cock before, though Judi didn't really know a cock; she only thought she did.

"Devil can never know."

"I'm not going to be telling your daddy what I want to do to you." He stroked her hair, tugging her head back exposing her neck. Ripper leaned down pressing his lips to her neck, biting down. "What's it going to be, Princess?"

She stayed silent for several minutes teasing him with a response. Sucking on the flesh of her neck, he made sure not to leave a mark. Devil would spot a hickey a mile away. What was going on between them? Ripper didn't have an answer. They'd always gravitated toward each other. He remembered more often than not Judi standing with him, talking and cooking while the others mingled.

Don't think. Feel.

"Yes, I want this, Ripper."

"Then you better tell me what you want. I'm not going to do anything you don't want." Both of his hands went to her hair, tugging on the length so she couldn't hide her response from him.

"I want you to kiss me."

Dropping down, he brushed his lips against her cheek. "Is that what you want, baby?"

"No, on my lips. I want you to kiss me like you mean it."

Smiling, he pressed his lips to hers, waiting for her response. Her hands landed on his arms, gripping his muscles. "There's no turning back."

"I know."

Gripping her head, he slammed his lips down on

hers, plunging his tongue into her waiting mouth. She gasped, opening her lips, and Ripper took full advantage. Judi met his tongue with her own, sliding them against each other.

With his hands on her hand, he only kissed her, not pressing his cock to her stomach.

She moaned, and he didn't let go. When he was sure she wouldn't move away, he slid his hands down to cup her fall ass. Judi was his, and part of him knew he was never letting her go.

****

Staring at her reflection Judi wondered if she could see a difference from the kiss alone. He'd dropped her off ten minutes ago, and she'd climbed the wall to get into her room. There was no sign of anyone in her room, and she'd quickly removed her clothes changing into her nightwear of shorts and a vest. Releasing her hair, she turned her face left and right. It was past one, and Ripper had spent a long time simply kissing her lips.

Pressing a finger to her lips she felt she could taste him on her tongue. He didn't stop kissing her until he was ready to stop. His touch was so demanding yet sweet at the same time.

You're losing your mind.

Switching the light off, she went to her bed and lay down staring at the ceiling. There was no way she'd be returning to college. She'd talk to Devil soon about changing to online classes rather than leaving him. Thinking about Devil, she did understand what Ripper was talking about. He'd become the father she never had. The club was her family, and no one messed with her. She knew the dynamics of the club. When they had gatherings with family members she saw all the sweet-butts and the men.

Judi refused to think about Ripper as anything

other than a friend with benefits. He wasn't the kind of man who settled down with a woman. She'd heard many of the sweet-butts talking about his needs within the bedroom. His attitude was also well known as being unapproachable. Ripper never treated her like that. They were always friendly with each other.

Rolling to her side she stared out of the window into the darkness. What would it be like to finally give herself to a man she actually wanted? Thumping her pillow she rolled over trying to get the kiss out of mind. Closing her eyes, she felt so tired and just wanted to sleep.

The following morning she woke up hearing Simon screaming. Getting to her feet she walked into the nursery to find Devil trying to change Elizabeth's diaper while also attempting to entertain Simon.

"Fuck, you stink, girl," Devil said.

Laughing, Judi walked into the room feeling really happy. "I'll help you out."

"Yeah, you take care of Elizabeth, and I'll get breakfast on," Devil said.

Picking Simon up, she shook her head. "You're dear old daddy. You can deal with her … mess."

Leaving the nursery Judi couldn't stop laughing all the way to the kitchen. She stopped to give Simon time on the toilet before getting him to wash his hands. "Your daddy is seeing the error of his ways in diapers."

Putting the kettle on, she placed some porridge in a bowl for Simon then watched as Devil came downstairs looking green.

She handed him a coffee before going back to the stove.

"What's for breakfast?" he asked.

"I'm making some scrambled eggs. I'm not doing anything with too much of a bad smell," she said, pointing up at the ceiling.

"I know. She slept all night last night. Everything in the books has said it's morning sickness and said it should go."

Judi served them both up breakfast, sitting at the counter staring at him. "Why do you think it's something different?"

"She didn't have this kind of illness with the other two."

"Other one," she said, pointing at Simon.

"Shit, yeah. I forget at times. She didn't have it with Elizabeth."

Simon was not Lexie's son. Her sister dropped him off within days of him being born to look after. Judi didn't know what had gone down between Lexie's sister, Kayla, and Devil, only that Kayla had never returned to take her son.

"No pregnancy is the same. Trust Lexie. She'll let you know when something is not right."

She ate her scrambled eggs and tried not to think about last night. Thoughts of Ripper's lips on her lips going down to her neck were invading her mind constantly.

"What did you do last night?" Devil asked.

"Erm, read a little. There's something I want to talk to you about actually. I was thinking of finishing my courses online. Lexie could do with the help, and I can learn the same here as I can at college." She stared into his eyes hoping he didn't notice the blush she was sure stained her cheeks.

"What's wrong with college?"

"Nothing. Lexie and Phoebe need me. I also know club business still goes down." She held her hand up to stop him from interfering. "The Skulls talk, and you do as well. I also notice you lock the door to your office. Don't lie to me, Devil. I'm not wanting part of it, but you can't be here twenty-four seven. What will happen if you're needed to help The Skulls out again?"

A couple of years ago, not long after she'd moved in with Devil and Lexie, he disappeared to help Tiny, the president of The Skulls, when he was under threat. The two clubs had formed some kind of friendship, and Lexie always catered to them when they visited.

"You know too much for your own good."

"Can I stay home?" she asked.

"You fall behind at college and I'll ground you," he said.

Judi burst out laughing. She'd never been grounded in her whole life. "You're kidding, right? I'm twenty years old."

"Yeah, I'm bigger, stronger, and pay for your college, Princess. I'll put you over my knee if I have to. You're my girl, remember?"

She knew she shouldn't find the threat of a spanking sweet, but she did. Devil had really taken the role of her father seriously.

"I love you, Devil."

"Love you, too, Princess."

There was no sexual love between them. They were like father and daughter.

"What have I missed?" Lexie asked, entering the kitchen. There was a little color in her cheeks for the first time since her pregnancy began.

"Nothing. I'm going to be sticking around for a while," Judi said, grabbing some plain toast for Lexie.

"Really, why?"

"Mommy," Simon said, reaching for Lexie.

"Leave her be, son," Devil said.

"I think it's best I stick around. You may not think you need me, Lex, but you do."

"I'm not going to lie. Your presence will be welcome, especially when Devil goes on one of his runs. I know you've left it to the boys. They need their leader with them, baby."

Judi watched the moment between the two without saying anything.

"I'm going to the library and get everything set up. I'll be back by twelve." Judi kissed Lexie on the cheek then moved to Devil doing the same. Once she was dressed she saw a text from Ripper waiting for her.

Ripper: What you doing today?
Judi: I'm going to the library.

Hiking her bag onto her shoulder she walked downstairs and said her goodbyes to Devil. She didn't mind walking into town. Her cell phone buzzed, and she saw it was from Ripper again.

Ripper: Meet me around the back.

What was he doing? Excitement filled every part of her senses. Even as she thought he was crazy, she couldn't stop the thrill of knowing she was going to see him again so soon. Walking into town she made her way around the back of the library to find Ripper there, smoking. He threw the cigarette away when he saw her.

Walking toward him she stopped with enough distance between them so no one would think anything of them being together. "What are you doing here?" she asked.

"I came to see you."

"I talked with Devil. I've got to get back home by twelve."

"I'm not here to detain you, baby. Come here and give me a kiss."

Her heart leapt inside her chest. Closing the distance between them, she wrapped her arms around his neck as he held onto her waist. His lips were on hers in the next second, and she felt like she was floating away from the pleasure of his lips alone.

"Fuck, I missed you last night," he said, muttering the words against her lips.

"We were only apart for a few hours."

"I couldn't stop thinking about your fucking lips. They're going to be the only thing I can think about."

Drawing him down, she licked along his full lips before plundering her tongue into his mouth. His hands squeezed her ass, and heat swamped her pussy.

"Right, I'm going to leave you to your work," he said, pulling away and forcing her away from him.

"What? You're just going to leave?"

"Yep, try and concentrate on your coursework not me." He stroked a finger down her cheek before leaving.

The bastard. He knew she wouldn't be able to focus on anything else but him.

Growling in annoyance she stormed into the library. Setting up her work online she sent the college an email then started to arrange for her course books to be sent home. All the time she worked, her lips tingled from the simple contact with Ripper.

Chapter Five

"Anyone know what's going on with Tiny and The Skulls?" Ripper asked. When he entered the clubhouse twenty minutes ago he'd discovered they were all in church talking. Devil had seemed satisfied with his excuse of needing a ride for not being at the club. He thought about Judi and the way her lips had quivered beneath his as he kissed her. Fuck, he couldn't get her off his mind.

"Tiny got in touch about a girl called Prue. She was shot and is in the hospital and critical. No one knows he's phoned me to give me an update," Devil said, running a finger over his lips.

"Who is Prue?" Curse asked.

"She's something to do with Zero. Tiny believes one of his boys is in danger. He's asked for our help if it's needed. At the moment, it's only Prue, and they don't know much else."

This was their time to bring ideas to the table and handle problems within the club.

"I could do with a ride. If Tiny needs us I'd be happy to back you and head to Fort Wills. I love watching The Skulls panic when we arrive," Curse said, speaking up first.

"The problem I have is Lexie. If shit goes down with her pregnancy or with the Princess I need people here." Devil looked around at each of them.

"I'll stay behind," Ripper said, speaking up.

All of the men turned to him. "I get my shit from driving up to the picnic space. I'm good to stay behind if you all need to get your shit handled." For an excuse it was a good one. He just couldn't imagine being away from Judi any time right now. Last night he hadn't gotten her out of his mind. This morning he couldn't think of anything else but the feel of her lips against his own.

"You sure?"

"Yeah, I'm sure," Ripper said. "Someone needs to stay behind, and I've got nothing pulling me away."

Curse was staring at him without saying a word.

"Then it's handled. If The Skulls need us then we go, and, Ripper, you stay with Vincent and a few others."

"I will." He nodded his head and the meeting moved on toward a drug deal with Jerry. Jerry was a pimp and drug dealer. He lived not too far from Devil but they struck a bargain two years ago when they moved to Piston County. They worked for each other and the profits were split fairly.

When the meeting was over he left to go to his room. Curse grabbed his arm and led him outside for some privacy.

"What the fuck do you want?" Ripper asked, wanting to get showered.

"We're friends, Ripper. What the fuck is going on?" Curse had his arms folded and wouldn't budge an inch.

"I don't know what the fuck you're talking about."

"Shall I go and tell Devil about the guy we buried then, or have you forgotten about him?" Curse turned to go to Devil.

Shit, there was no way he was going to let that happen.

"It was Judi's kill, okay. She called me for help, not fucking Devil." Ripper let the words tumble out of his mouth.

"Judi? What the fuck was she doing out?" Curse asked, looking angry.

"I don't know. She wanted to walk and get some air or some shit. I didn't ask the bitch too many questions. I took care of it."

"She killed someone, Ripper. Shit like that doesn't go away."

"I'm handling it."

He fisted his hands, and Curse kept staring at him.

"You better. Judi is precious to all of us."

Ripper kept his mouth shut. If he said anything more Curse would know the truth of his change of feelings toward the woman they considered a Princess.

"Is there anything else you're not telling me?" Curse asked.

"Nothing. I've got everything handled." Ripper thought about the passion he experienced from Judi's lips alone. She felt the same way. He had seen the budding of her nipples at their kiss.

The life she'd led before he turned up didn't affect him. Judi may have had over one hundred men, but no man ever got into her heart or mind. The fact she'd remained whole throughout her experience was a surprise. Many women would have broken a long time ago. There were strippers at the club who were similar in age but looked years older than Judi's twenty years.

"If you need anything else, let me know. I'll do anything for our Princess."

Nodding, Ripper lit up a cigarette looking for some way to change the conversation away from Judi. "What was wrong with you yesterday at the diner? Mia was taking an order, and you looked like she was begging for your cock."

Curse took his cigarette from him. "Nothing."

"Really, nothing. So you weren't imagining your cock deep inside her cunt?"

The other man shook his head. "Stick to fucking with women. I'm out of here." Curse left him alone.

Seconds later he heard the sound of Curse's bike purring to life. Leaning against the back of the wall of the club Ripper tried to gather his thoughts together.

You should put an end to this shit with Judi. The club is far more important than some bitch.

Taking a deep draw on his cigarette he closed his eyes and rubbed them to try to clear his mind.

She's not yours to have, to touch, or to fuck.

"I appreciate you staying behind if the shit hits the fan," Devil said.

Opening his eyes, Ripper saw his leader stood beside him. "No problem. I don't mind sticking around for the girls." Staring down at his feet, the torment started to build back up inside him. Judi was off limits to men like him.

"I don't want to ruin shit. Judi is happier than I've ever seen her. Lexie is ill, but life still keeps on going." Devil lit up a cigarette.

Chancing a glance at his president, Ripper saw the pain in Devil's eyes.

"You're not going to lose Lexie."

"I know. Until you've got a woman pregnant, Ripper, don't say anything more."

He wished there was something more he could say. At thirty-three years old, Ripper had been through hell, but his loyalty to Devil was absolute.

Your loyalty means shit. You're going to fuck with Judi.

She deserves better than you.

"I can't speak from experience of having kids. My dick has always got a rubber on it, but Lexie will not let anything happen to her."

Devil didn't say anything.

"She became a stripper for Simon. If a woman who is as reserved as Lexie is at times, still took her clothes off to earn money, she won't put herself in danger for your kid."

"I don't give a fuck about my kid. Do you think I want any brat around me if they're responsible for killing her?" Devil shouted the words.

The sound of a gasp came from behind him. Lexie stood there, pale, and stared at him.

"Shit, baby, I'm so sorry." Devil went to Lexie, who turned to walk away. Rubbing at his eyes, Ripper knew he'd fucked up talking to his boss. Shit, he shouldn't have said anything, and Lexie shouldn't have turned up. Leaving the clubhouse, which reminded him a lot of the building in Fort Wills, he rounded the building to see Lexie shouting at Devil. In all fairness, Devil looked ready to pick her up and take her away like some kind of caveman.

"I've got morning sickness, Devil. When are you going to get it through your thick fucking skull?" Lexie asked, shouting.

"You were not this way with Elizabeth."

"Newsflash, jerk, I'm not pregnant with Elizabeth."

Ripper climbed on his bike leaving them to their argument. Several of the women were laughing. The last thing he saw was Devil shutting her up with his mouth. Yep, that's the only way to keep a woman silent these days.

He entered town going to the library. The librarian clucked her tongue at him. Chuckling, he looked through the rooms until he found Judi sitting at one computer typing away. For several minutes he stood watching her with his arms folded. She looked distracted reading through each line then checking out some fact in one of the books. Two guys close to her age were chuckling and pointing over at her.

Ripper didn't like the look on their faces and took the seat beside her. "Hey, Princess," he said, raising his voice so all could hear.

"What are you doing here?" she asked.

Her cheeks went a beautiful shade of red. Leaning forward, he brushed a strand of hair out of his way to watch her. "I thought I'd come and see you. Devil and Lexie were arguing about her morning sickness when I left them at the club. I thought I'd come and see what you're doing." Ripper wanted to do so much more than touch.

"I should be getting my course books in the post in the next couple of weeks. When they turn up I'm good to go. I just need to get this assignment done and I can have a few days off."

Getting to his feet, Ripper smiled down at her. "Then go ahead, write. I'm going to look around." He was going to threaten the two dipshits with his gun, but she didn't need to know that.

"Okay." Her attention was already back on the computer.

Now, he could go and take his anger out on the two men who were pointing at his woman.

****

Typing the last few sentences, Judi rubbed the back of her neck working out the kinks. She'd been staring at her computer screen for the last couple of hours, and she was feeling the strain on her eyes. Ripper still hadn't left. Lexie and Devil phoned her earlier to make sure she was okay. They told her to get her assignment finished before returning home.

"Are you done?" Ripper asked, suddenly appearing behind her.

She'd been aware of two boys pointing and giggling hours earlier, but something must have happened because they left the building looking pale.

"Yeah, I just finished up." Judi stretched out, her muscles moaning. Pressing the necessary keys she stood up going to the printer. She would have to read through it before sending it back to her tutor. Filing the assignment away, she pushed some hair out of her face then closed the computer down. "I'm so tired."

Her stomach chose that moment to growl.

"Hungry as well," Ripper said, chuckling.

"Are you laughing at me?" She tensed, feeling her cheeks heat at the noise her body made.

"No, I'm not laughing at you. It's a good job I've got plenty of money to feed you." He took her hand as she placed the strap of her bag on her shoulder. Before she said anything he was leading her out of the room toward the diner opposite the library.

"Are you always this bossy?" she asked, getting annoyed at him taking charge.

Not annoyed, turned on.

Cutting the thought off, she followed behind him with no choice as he held her hand. They were seated in the back of the diner and looking over the menu within seconds.

"Yes, I'm bossy. I like shit done my way. Besides, what would you have done for food?" he asked.

"I'd have gone home to eat."

"Yeah, probably waited until dinner and survived on a piece of fruit. Women, fucking lunatics."

"What the hell is that supposed to mean?" she asked. Her anger sparked at his condescending attitude.

"We live one life, and you're always so fussy about what goes in your mouth. Food is fucking food. Enjoy it and relish it."

"It's easy to say coming from a guy who can eat whatever the hell he wants." She folded her arms, glaring at him.

"I take great pains to keep my body in shape."

"Fucking every woman you come across, I'm surprised you're not anorexic." There was a time before Lexie when she'd been slender, underweight even. Now she had curves in all the wrong places.

"Are you jealous?" he asked. There was a wicked smile on his face. She hated him.

"No, I'm not jealous. You're a walking, talking advert for sexual diseases." She picked up the menu, lifting it in front of her face so she didn't have to look at Ripper's smug looking bastard face. In that instant she hated him and everything he stood for.

Ripper quickly moved, sitting beside her. She was trapped against the wall and his hard body. "What's the matter, baby? Do I get you all hot?" He placed a hand in between her thighs right against her pussy.

She gasped. The heat of him landed where she most needed him. "What are you doing?" she asked, glancing around the diner. No one was paying them any attention. No one would even know his hand was on her mound.

"I'm looking at your menu. I shooed the waitress away. There's only me and you." He didn't move his hand away.

Closing her eyes, she tried to focus on something that wasn't him. "This shouldn't be happening."

Her panties were soaking wet against her skin. She was sure of it. The torture of his hand was driving her insane. His lips were so close to her neck.

"I love your curves, Judi. You were too fucking thin when we first met. This is much better. I will boss you around because it's fun and I enjoy it. I imagine there is going to come a time when you will, too."

Suddenly his hand was gone, and she was left

alone where he had sat once before. Licking her lips, she tucked some hair behind her ear as the waitress approached. Mia smiled at each of them. "What can I get you both?"

Ripper ordered for both of them. Smiling, Judi closed the menu and waited for the woman to leave.

"Why did you do that? Was it some kind of control thing?" she asked.

"I did it because I wanted to."

"You know Devil would kill you if he knew," she said, not knowing why she brought him into their conversation.

"Any time you want to tell I'll be ready." He didn't avoid her gaze but looked directly at her.

"Don't you care?" she asked.

"I care. I shouldn't be touching you or be anywhere near you."

Tears filled her eyes at the dark look in his eyes. "Then why are you?" She was so confused.

"I can't stay away from you."

Biting her lip she looked down at the table in front of her. Her stomach growled, but she ignored the need to eat. "Have you tried to stay away from me?"

"More than you know."

She stayed silent as Mia brought food to the table. Judi had never felt happier at having a reason to eat. The conversation was scaring her a little. Ripper was a good friend to her, and she didn't want any hurt to come to him.

"I won't say anything to Devil. I don't even know why I said anything. Just ignore me." She picked up her burger and started eating.

Neither of them spoke. Ripper looked tormented as his gaze stayed on her. Her cell phone buzzed, and she placed the burger down to answer.

Lexie was calling.

"Hello," Judi said, answering. She tried to sound happy as she spoke to her friend.

"Judi, how are you doing?"

"I'm fine. I'm eating lunch with Ripper." She wasn't going to lie.

"Good. I wanted to let you know Devil is taking us out and wanted to know if you wanted to come. He's driving us out to a spa for a couple of days." Lexie sounded so excited.

"No, I'm going to pass. I've got a lot of work planned to catch up on."

"Are you sure?" Lexie asked.

"Yeah, I'll stay at the house. Don't worry about me. I can take care of myself."

"I know you can take care of yourself. Are you sure? We can have some fun." If Devil was taking Lexie and the kids to a spa, Judi knew he had every intention of them being looked after while he spent hours making love to her. There was no way she was going to be cramping his style.

"I'll pass. Maybe another time." Her heart was racing as Ripper stared at her, waiting.

What was going on in his head?

"Tell Ripper that Devil wants a word," Lexie said.

She handed the phone across the table. He didn't avert his gaze as Devil spoke. "I'll keep her protected. Yeah, spare bedroom sounds good."

Ripper ended the call, pocketing her phone.

"Hey, I need that."

"Eat up." He didn't give her back her phone.

"What's going on?" she asked.

"We're spending a few days together. Devil has already told the club I'm with you. We won't be disturbed." Ripper's gaze slid down her body.

For the last two years any man who looked at her like that would send her scampering away. Ripper made her burn brighter than ever before. Licking her lips, she took a bite out of her burger knowing it wasn't what she wanted to eat.

Neither of them spoke again. Ripper paid for their lunch. Within minutes they were back on his bike and riding toward her home. The car was gone from the lot, and when she entered she found the house incredibly empty.

Entering the kitchen she found an envelope on the counter. Inside was a note for her from Lexie including numbers and also plenty of money for her.

"With the way they treat me people would think I'm a child," Judi said.

"Like I said, Devil has taken on the daddy role, and there's no going back. As far as he's concerned, you're his little girl, and that's never going to change." His hand gripped the back of her neck.

The moment he touched her, her body went into overdrive. She couldn't think as his fingers stroked across her skin.

"I'm breaking so many rules you don't even know," he said, brushing his lips against her cheek.

Her heart was pounding with each touch. "Then stop," she said, hoping he didn't.

"I can't stop, Judi." Ripper spun her around to face him. "There is no turning back for me."

She stared up into his eyes seeing the green depths sparkle with his need. He pressed her against the counter. His cock rubbed her stomach. Judi gasped. Ripper was long, thick, and rock hard.

"Tell me to fuck off, Judi, and I will. I will never hurt you. You'll like everything I do to you."

Licking her lips, Judi knew there was no going back for either of them.

Chapter Six

Judi's arms circled his neck, and Ripper was completely lost. He lifted her up until her ass settled onto the counter. The jeans she wore were in the way of what he wanted, but gripping her head he took possession of her lips instead. She melted against him, moaning into his mouth.

Plunging his tongue between her lips, he tasted her and wanted more. He was a dying man, and the only thing left for him was her. Picking her up, he carried her across the hallway and made his way up to her bedroom. The only time he stopped was to press her against the wall and make love to her mouth. Her legs were wrapped around his waist, and he rubbed his cock against her core. The moment their clothes were gone, both of them were going to be screaming for more.

Devil was gone for a few days giving Ripper alone time with Judi. If he believed in God, he would think his prayers had been answered. He didn't believe in anything but his gut and his bike. Both never failed him. Even now his head was telling him to get the fuck out while his gut was sticking to fucking Judi.

Slamming her door closed, he placed her on her feet.

"Last chance, Princess."

"I'm not going anywhere," she said.

"Good." Dropping his jacket to the floor, he rid his body of his shoes and shirt, leaving his jeans on. Through it all he watched Judi getting undressed. Her hands were shaking, and he took over removing her clothing for her. She tried to cover her body, but he captured her hands holding them by her side.

"Fuck, you're something else." He held her hands out by her side and stared down at her full body. His cock was rock hard at the sight. Ripper was still in his jeans, and the tightness was unbearable. Her tits were large with tiny red nipples. He could fit one whole nipple into his mouth. They were fucking heavenly to look at. Her stomach was rounded and her hips flared out.

Her legs were nice and thick and could take a pounding. "Get on the bed," he said.

Going to his belt, he released his jeans, taking his time to move the fabric over his enlarged cock. He sprang free, and her eyes widened at the sight.

Climbing onto the bed, he shut out all thought of why he shouldn't be doing this.

"I'll give you one last chance, Princess," he said, settling between her thighs.

"I don't want you to go."

"I'm clean."

"So am I. I got tested when Devil took me in." He pressed his palm over her mouth, stopping her from talking.

"I know you're clean, baby. I've got condoms, but I wanted you to know I'm careful with my dick."

Leaning down, he took her lips, plunging his tongue into her mouth. She moaned, her nails scoring his back as he kissed his way down her body.

He took one nipple into his mouth, biting down onto the rock hard bud. Judi arched up to meet him. She tasted so fucking sweet. Moving to the next nipple, he circled the bud then went back to the first. When he was satisfied with the hardness of her nipples, he kissed down her stomach coming to just above her mound.

She had a nicely trimmed thatch of hair. He slid his fingers over, brushing the fine hairs. Her legs opened wide, and he smelled her arousal wafting up.

Ripper opened the lips of her sex to find her swollen clit glinting at him. The nub looked like a precious jewel. Using the tip of his finger, he caressed the nub watching her explode from the slightest bit of pressure.

"My Princess is so responsive and tender."

She screamed. Her whole body shook underneath his touch. Ripper stared up her body watching her tits quiver with her indrawn breaths. He closed the distance, covering her clit with his lips. Sucking the little jewel into his mouth, he held Judi down with hands on her hips. Sucking, flicking, and licking the tight little bud, Ripper held Judi in place while he made her come apart in his arms. Her pussy was on fire, and he intended to spend the rest of the day and night watching her splinter apart from his touch alone.

After her first orgasm, he pulled away wiping her cream from his face.

Her gaze was on his face with tears in her eyes. Ripper was determined to show her what making love was all about. All of his life he'd fucked women, rarely making love as that was about the connection between two people. Part of Judi's mind was broken, shattered over what her life had been for a few short years. He saw how little respect she had for men apart from the club men. They never held her past against her nor did they force her to give them something. She really was a princess in all of their eyes.

"I've, erm, I've never—" Judi stopped wiping the tears from her eyes. Crawling up the bed, Ripper wrapped his arms around her shoulders and drew her in close.

"Sh, you don't need to say anything to me. I'm not going to force you or make you do something you don't want." He kissed her head, knowing he would kill every last fucker who had touched her if it would take the sadness from her eyes. Judi was everything he wanted to protect.

"It's not you. I've never felt anything so amazing before in my life. I never knew it could … be that way." Her tears were falling thick and fast.

Holding her tighter, Ripper made a deal with himself that he would kill any man who had touched her in the past. If he so much as saw fear in her eyes he was going to annihilate them.

"It can be that way, baby. There can also be so much more. Your body, given the chance, can come alive in ways you've only ever dreamed of."

"I'm afraid, Ripper."

He tightened his arms around her. "I'll hold you throughout, baby. No one will ever harm you, I promise."

"I don't deserve you."

Gripping her cheek, he stared into her eyes feeling his anger close. "You deserve fucking better than me. I'm a fucking biker, Judi. I've fucked more women than you ever have men. I didn't care about anyone but the club until you. You make *me* want to be fucking better."

Running a hand down her body, he kept his gaze on her at all times. "You're fucking perfection whereas I'm a monster in comparison. I wish I could give you the kind words and all that shit, but I can't. I've only got what I am."

She touched his cheek, and her fingers heated his skin. He never wanted her to not want him. Judi was beautiful, sweet, and her eyes held a lifetime of pain. Given the chance he would replace that pain with love, happiness, and everything to make a woman's heart soar.

Judi smiled up at him with tears still in her eyes. "Be careful, Ripper. Anyone would think you've got words of love inside you." Her fingers moved to his lips, running the tips over him. "There's no one else I'd rather be with than with you."

Taking hold of her fingers, he sucked the digits into his mouth loving the gasp that left her lips at his touch. Each finger he sucked inside his mouth relishing the chance of tasting her. The sweet juice of her cream still in his mouth, he ran his fingers up and down her body. Her skin was soft to the touch.

"Please," she said, moaning.

Covering her lips with his own, he plundered her mouth with his tongue. "That's it, baby. Open up for me. Give me what I want."

She opened her lips, and their kiss deepened. His heart pounded as lust started to take over. He felt her hands running down his stomach tracing the rock hard abs before gripping his length. Hissing, he pulled away to watch her pale fingers pumping his cock.

"Be careful, baby. I'm so close to fucking coming, I'm not going to last."

"I think it's only fair."

Ripper wanted to be deep inside her cunt, but if this was what she wanted to do their first time he was more than happy about it. Gazing down at her full body, his cock tightened painfully. Her body was curvy in all the right places.

She fisted his cock creating a steady pace. He took several deep breaths not wanting to go over the edge too soon. In many respects this was Judi's first real time. All of the other times she'd been with the men had been paying for a release. This time was about their mutual pleasure. Ripper wanted to hear her come apart just as much as he wanted to feel his own orgasm.

"Am I doing this right?" she asked.

Pressing his head to hers, Ripper chuckled. "Baby, you're doing everything fucking right."

Ripper claimed her lips as she worked his cock.

The tightness of her fingers was driving him crazy. He cupped her cheeks, tilting her head back to deepen the kiss. Her breathing increased going to shallow pants.

Thrusting his hips up against her hands Ripper felt himself getting close to his release. Growling, he tightened his hands on her hips as she worked his cock.

"I'm coming, baby," he said, panting.

The first drops of his cum coated her stomach. His release spurted between them covering them both.

She didn't stop until he stilled her movements with his hand. "You need to stop, baby, while I've got some sanity left." Fuck, that one orgasm alone was so fucking perfect that all others paled in comparison.

****

Judi stared up into his beautiful green eyes. Her heart pounded, and she didn't care that she was covered in his cum. That one moment together meant more to her than the hundred she spent with other men. His hand remained over hers. She was shocked by the heat of his touch.

"Wow," he said, drawing her attention to his lips, which were amazing to feel against her own.

"What?" she asked, wanting to hear his voice.

"You're going to be the death of me, woman."

"You're the one who made a mess." She released his cock to finger the white droplets coating her skin.

He chuckled. "Time for a shower I think." Ripper got up from the bed then picked her up. "We'll take care of the sheets once we're cleaned."

Judi gasped as he carried her through to the bathroom. This was her space, and she'd never be able to look at it the same way again. She watched as he turned the shower on testing the water for the heat. Glancing in the mirror she was shocked by the total contrast of the pair of them. She was pale as she didn't go out in the sun all that much. Keeping her body covered was all she cared about. Ripper was dark from working in the sun. His body was rock hard whereas she was soft, curvy.

Turning away from the mirror she saw Ripper was watching her. He moved behind her, circling her body with his arms. Together they looked at their reflections. "Do you have any idea how fucking sexy you are?" he asked.

She shook her head glancing down at his hands.

"You make me so fucking hot for you." He pressed his cock against her ass. She felt he was already thickening at that simple touch. "We're taking this one step at a time."

"Okay."

"Let's get washed," he said, taking her hand and leading her into the shower.

Judi would have slipped if not for his hold on her body.

"Thank you," she said.

"When are you going to learn I'm always going to be here to catch you?" He kissed her neck, and she swallowed against the lump in her throat. His entire presence took her by surprise. Ripper would say something that left her completely speechless.

He pressed her toward the front with a hand on her shoulder. She looked up at the water, closing her eyes to let the warmth seep into her bones.

Ripper's hands held the soap as he started to work the lather against her skin.

"I can wash myself," she said, going to turn around. He stopped her, tightening his grip on her shoulder to keep her in place. Licking her lips, she stayed still as he soaped her body.

"I'm going to do what I want," he said, working the soap down her back. When his hands were covered in soap he used them to wash her body. She gasped as he paid careful attention to her breasts then between her legs. "I've got to get you all nice and clean. I can't have you feeling dirty."

Once all the soap was off his hands she expected him to take his turn. That was not the case. His hands rubbed against her skin, taking his time almost as if to memorize her shape. Up his hands went to cup her tits. His thumb pressed on her nipples then pinched them creating a spark of pleasure that took her completely by surprise.

She whimpered.

"Are you nice and wet for me, Judi?" he asked, whispering the words against her ear.

Jerking her head, she had no choice but to stand in his arms waiting.

"I didn't hear you."

"I'm wet," she said, crying out.

One of his palms cupped her pussy. She felt him slide between her folds, going down to sink a finger inside her.

"Fuck, baby, you're fucking wet." A second finger was added inside her stretching her out. "You're tight as well. I'm a big man, baby. I've got to make sure you can fit me inside your tight little cunt." He pumped his fingers in and out of her pussy. Each delicious pump of his hand made it hard for her to concentrate. There was a burning sensation from being stretched from his fingers alone.

From the moment Devil entered her life she'd not been with a man since. She didn't touch herself or invite men to think anything else. Judi had kept them at arms' length until Ripper. There was so much more she wanted from him but couldn't find the right words to tell him what she really wanted.

"Do you always talk?" she asked. His words were not offending her. They turned her on. He had one of those voices that struck her hard, melting her.

"Baby, I want the woman I'm with to know what I want. Get used to me talking, telling you what I like."

She whimpered as another finger penetrated her pussy.

"Get used to this pussy being fucked. When you let me inside your body, Judi, I know I'm going to be in heaven. You'll give me everything and take everything I've got to give you." He worked his fingers in and out. Her cream lubricated his movements. Biting her lip, she reached out to the wall to hold herself up. Palms flat, she felt his body still pressed firmly behind her. "Your pussy is going to be like heaven. I'm never going to be able to find pleasure anywhere else. Will you give me your pussy whenever I need to fuck?" he asked.

She closed her eyes, thinking about what he said. There was a time the thought of sex repulsed her, but not anymore. Her body was on fire for Ripper and his brand of sex.

"Please," she said, moaning as his thumb pressed to her clit.

"Do you want to come over my fingers, baby? Do I get to feel your cream soaking my fingers?"

Words failed her as her body took over demanding to be heard.

"Come on, Judi, give me your orgasm. Let me hear you scream."

Nothing else mattered. Her past fell away, and the only people left in the world were her and Ripper.

"Trust me, baby. I'll be here to catch you, always."

His thumb stroked over her nub, and her orgasm crashed over her, taking her breath away. Her grip on the wall held her up.

"That's it, Judi. I can feel your cream coating my fingers. Give me your cum."

Ripper's words tore into her soul leaving nothing in its place. She never thought she'd be able to have something like this with anyone else. Every word that left his lips opened her up to more.

"Such a good girl. Give me it all." His touch didn't stop until he was satisfied.

Slowly, he moved his hand away holding her hips.

"Now it's your turn to wash me." He took her place standing under the water. She picked up the soap then started to touch his skin. His back was covered in tattoos. None of them really stood out. His flesh was a work of art.

"Do you have a thing for needles?" she asked, caressing down his back.

"I love feeling the bite in my skin."

The designs were amazing, beautiful, and breathtaking, like the male. His hair darkened from the water. She soaped his back and ass going to her knees to do his feet. She stepped to the side to wash his front. Any chance she got to look at him she would take.

His cock was thrust out, long, thick and pulsed to life. Her hands shook as she did his chest working her way down to his cock.

"How can you be ready to go again?" she asked, shocked by the strength of his arousal.

"You. You make me want to fuck you, Judi."

Soaping his length, she heard him moan. Seconds later his fingers circled hers around his shaft, and he showed her the pace he wanted her to keep. Her fingers were tight as she worked his length.

"I'm going to come," he said.

Judi kept up her ministrations watching the tip as his cum jerked out, splashing onto the bottom of the shower, washing down the drain.

Once they were finished, Ripper turned the water off grabbing a towel for himself. She made to climb out, but he wrapped a towel around her body.

"Are you sure you're a bad-ass biker?" she asked.

"Yes."

He was being sweet to her, and she didn't understand where his tough image came from. Thinking about the dead body, she closed the thoughts down. Ripper was a force to be reckoned with. She doubted anyone got to see this side of him.

"Don't mistake my caring for you as a weakness, Judi. Only you will see this side of me and only in private." He kissed her cheek then took her hand leading her back to her bedroom.

"I'm hungry."

She was shocked to see they'd been in her bedroom for two hours already. The time didn't even register when they were together.

Chapter Seven

Sitting at the kitchen counter, Ripper watched Judi buzzing around the spacious kitchen. She wore a pair of shorts and a vest. He wouldn't let her have a bra or panties, and he liked the view of watching her tits bounce as she moved. His cock was in pain at the jeans he wore, but he wasn't prepared to walk around buck ass naked yet.

"Do you mind having spicy chicken with salad?" she asked, holding up a plate with lots of chicken breasts on it.

"Make sure you cook all of that," he said.

"What? There's a lot here."

"Baby, I eat a lot, and chicken and salad is not going to cut it."

"Okay, I'll make something to go with it."

Watching her move around the kitchen, he took a sip of his coffee while also thinking about her tight cunt squeezing the life out of his fingers. Her body was going to give him a walking, talking hard-on.

The shower alone had him bursting at the seams. He didn't shower with a woman. Ripper fucked women, and once he was done, they left his space. Judi was different. She made him want to be a different kind of man for her.

Running fingers through his hair he stood up going to look outside of the window. The sun was still bright in the sky. The neighborhood was a good one. He watched kids playing on the front lawns. All of them were wearing buttoned up shirts and looked out of place shooting hoops.

"How do you like living here?" he asked.

"It's good. We're left alone. Lexie won't take any shit from any of the women, and the men are terrified of

Devil." She giggled, looking over at him. "Lexie went to grab the mail the other day from the post box at the end of the drive, and one of the guys who lives a few doors down was passing with his dog." Her eyes were twinkling as she spoke. "He was flirting with Lexie. His hands reached out as if to touch her, and Devil lost it. He stormed out of the house and threatened him with his gun. Pretty much said if he didn't stick to his own pussy, he wouldn't have a dick left."

"That makes you laugh?" Ripper asked, smiling.

She didn't smile enough. He made a mental note to change that. Judi was only twenty, and she should be having all kinds of experiences to make her laugh and smile.

"Yeah, what I enjoyed was the shock on his face. All of the people think they're so good, better than everyone else, but none of them gave a shit about others. Devil is the president of an MC, and yet he cares. I don't know. Maybe I'm just sick in the head that watching rich people being threatened gives me a thrill." She shrugged her shoulders. He watched her place the chicken onto an oven plate and drizzle it with oil. Ripper loved deep fried food but wasn't prepared for another argument from her lips.

"They didn't care enough to stop a pimp like Rob from hurting you," Ripper said.

Judi paused. Her hand started to shake, and she looked up at him and nodded. "Yeah, they didn't care at all."

"What actually happened?" Ripper asked. They knew she ended up in Rob's clutches, but no one knew why. "You don't have to tell me if you're not comfortable." He wouldn't hold anything against her.

"It's the past. I always try to forget about the past." She put the chicken in the oven and turned back to him. Her breasts were rock hard and caught his attention.

He heard her blow out a breath.

"I was an only child, and when my parents died suddenly in a car crash I ended up living with an aunt. She was a bad person. A real piece of work so that even my parents didn't visit her or have anything to do with her." She pushed some hair out of her face, looking past his shoulder. "She hated that I cost her money, and when Rob appeared with one of his whores in the neighborhood she told him to take me away and that she'd make excuses. I don't know what happened to her. When I tried to get away she was already gone. He caught me, and I learned life was easier not to run and to just do as I was told. I was with him for over a year and a half before you guys showed up."

He saw her shaking.

Going over to her, he wrapped his arms around her body, holding her close.

"What's your aunt's name?" he asked.

She gave him the name, and he put it away for later use. "I'm sorry. I don't want you to feel sorry for me. Devil and the Chaos Bleeds crew came, and I'm here." She shrugged, smiling. "I'm fine now. The past is in the past. It can't hurt me anymore."

Ripper was going to make sure it never hurt her again.

"While you make the salad I'm going to go and make a call. I just remembered some business. The doors are locked." He left her alone going out the back yard toward the pool. Tugging out his cell phone, he checked to see if he had the number he needed.

Dialing, he stared at the pool wondering if he could convince Judi to take a swim with him sometime.

"What up?" Whizz asked.

Whizz was the computer genius who rode with

The Skulls. Whoever needed information went to him.

"I need to find someone, but I don't want anyone to know I'm looking."

"Oh, covert shit I can do. It's a piece of piss," Whizz said.

There was laughter and feminine moans in the background.

"Quiet down, bitches. I'm working here." Whizz yelled in the background. "Sorry, I'm having my own personal fuck-fest party. What can I do for you?"

Ripper gave the name. "I want to know where she is. Don't tell anyone else what you're doing. This is personal."

"It shouldn't take me long," Whizz said.

"Let me know everything you've got when you're done."

"Will do."

He hung up looking down at the pool. Minutes later Judi came out carrying a plate of food. "Dinner is served."

When Whizz came through, Ripper was going to take care of the bitch who'd hurt Judi. The aunt was living on borrowed fucking time, and he'd take great pleasure in hurting her before he finally killed her.

****

Washing up the dishes, Judi looked out over the front lawn. The last few hours had been magical. Ripper kept trying to get her to have a swim, and she refused finally lying and giving him the excuse that she didn't have a costume.

While she did the dishes, cleaning away all of her mess, he had disappeared upstairs. She didn't ask him where he was going. Wiping her hands on the towel she turned around to see Ripper standing with pieces of string dangling off his finger.

"What are they?" she asked, knowing he'd found something for her to wear.

"Lexie is similar in size to you. She's got more than enough costumes for you to wear. If I can't get you to go naked then you're wearing this." He laid each piece on the counter for her to get a good look at.

"You're insane if you think I'm going to wear something Lexie has worn. I love her and she's one of my closest friends, but even I draw the line of wearing something so personal." She folded her arms, feeling like she'd won.

Ripper wasn't going to get her into a bikini or any costume.

He smiled and produced a tag. "Good, I'm sure she won't mind you wearing one of her new ones. She's got a lot waiting to be used."

"You bastard," she said.

"Language, baby. I'll take you over my knee and spank that ass if you start bad-mouthing me." He picked up the bra bikini and approached her. She folded her arms over her breasts, glaring at him.

"I'm not getting in that thing."

"Yes, you are."

"Why should I?" she asked.

His hands stroked up either side of her arms. "Because you want to please me. Seeing you in this and taking a dip in the pool will please me."

"I don't want to please you." She gasped as his hand went between her thighs, stroking up the inside of her thigh. His fingers worked under the bottom of her shorts going to the evidence of what his closeness was doing to her. She gasped as his fingers went to her pussy, sliding between her folds and touching her clit.

"Baby, the only person you're denying is yourself. You want to please me, and taking a swim before I take you back to your room and eat your pussy is what will make me happy." He kissed her neck, sucking on her pulse.

"This is not fair."

He grabbed her hand and pressed her palm to his dick. "What's not fair is you teasing me with your sweet cunt. I want to see you in this costume and having fun." He dropped a kiss to her lips. "Is that too much to ask?"

Looking up at him, she dropped her arms from her breasts. "No, it's not too much to ask." She spoke the words through gritted teeth. "I don't like you right now."

"I don't need you to like me. I can feel your pussy likes me so much more."

He grabbed the bottom of her shirt and pulled it over her head. She stood still as he worked the cups over her breasts then tied the string around her neck to her back.

Glaring at him, she held onto the counter as he tugged down her shorts. He didn't grab the panties immediately to put on her. Glancing down at him, she saw he was staring at her pussy.

"What's the matter?" she asked.

Ripper didn't answer. He lifted one of her legs onto her shoulder as he closed the distance sliding his tongue deep into her cunt. She cried out at the sudden change. His tongue plunged into her core before sliding up to stroke her clit. Several times he did this before he released her leg.

In no time at all, she had on the bikini, and he arranged it to his liking.

"There, you're ready for a swim."

She didn't avert her gaze as he pushed the jeans off his body. He wore a pair of black boxer briefs, which clearly outlined his large cock.

"Are you sure you want to be swimming with

that?" she asked, pointing at his large erection. "You'll drown."

Ripper started to laugh. "I'm not drowning. I'll take care of my dick all in good time." She liked it when he took her hand and led her out toward the swimming pool. Tucking some hair behind her ear, she still felt a little self-conscious of her weight. His reaction to her body filled her with a little more confidence than she thought she possessed.

Suddenly, he stopped, turned and picked her up.

"What the hell are you doing?" she asked, screaming as he ran the last few steps and chucked her into the pool.

Screaming, Judi broke the surface, gasping for breath and laughing. Looking around the pool she tried to find him. When she got her hands on him, she was going to hurt him, maybe twist his balls right clear off.

Wiping the water from her eyes, she couldn't find him. Her feet were yanked from under her, catching her unaware. Arms flailing out each side she screamed as arms circled her waist, pulling her close.

Ripper was laughing down at her.

"You bastard," she said, slapping his chest. Judi wasn't afraid. She just didn't find what he'd done all that funny. "I could have drowned."

"Do you really think I'd let anything happen to you?" he asked.

She held onto his shoulders, glaring at him. "It wasn't fair."

"No? Then why are you smiling?"

Judi frowned, realizing she had in fact been laughing in between screaming. She wasn't panicked or scared and in fact, felt … exhilarated.

"You can thank me any time now."

"I don't like how you start having fun," she said,

moving away from him. The cool water felt good on her skin after the heat of the sun. Not only was the heat of the sun bothering her but also Ripper. His presence alone set a fire deep inside her that she didn't think she'd ever be able to put out. His words, everything about him, set her aflame.

He stepped toward her, and she stepped back. They did this until her back met the edge of the pool. "Baby, I'm always about having fun." Ripper cupped her cheeks, tilting her head back before claiming her lips.

As she melted against him, all was forgiven for throwing her into the pool.

If she didn't know any better, she'd start to think she was falling in love with the hard man.

"That's better. I like you all quiet and compliant. It makes me think I'm getting my own way." He squeezed one of her breasts before swimming away.

Feeling raw and exposed by the thoughts running through her head, she started swimming without looking at him. Judi needed to get her body and mind under control.

Falling in love with Ripper would be a big mistake. One, they hadn't agreed to anything at all. She knew without a doubt that he'd never settle down for one woman. He loved women and sex, and she knew enough that she wouldn't be able to satisfy all of his needs.

At one end of the pool she turned and started her laps toward the other end of the pool. Her time with Rob had taught her no man stayed faithful forever. She watched Devil with Lexie and she hoped he was an exception, but part of her really believed he would stray from his wife soon enough.

"What's going on in that mind of yours?" Ripper asked, snatching her around the waist and turning her to face him.

He was handsome in a weird kind of way. She liked his red hair, his muscles, and the hard eyes that stared back at her.

"Nothing."

"You're closed down. I don't like it. What's going on?"

"Nothing." She couldn't think of any other words to pacify him.

"Don't lie to me."

Throwing her hands up in the air, Judi let everything out. "I was thinking about Devil, and I know that he's not going to stay faithful to Lexie all that long. Men cannot be faithful. Men cheat, and they hurt the ones they love the most." She made sure to keep her growing feelings for Ripper locked up inside.

For several seconds he didn't say anything. His arms held her tightly, but his eyes seemed to shut down, going hard. What was he thinking?

Chapter Eight

Should he spank her ass inside the house or by the side of the pool? Ripper wasn't sure in which room to punish her. He knew he was going to spank her ass for the shit she'd just talked about, and once he was done they were going to have a bloody good talking to. The shit that spewed from her mouth needed to stop. Hauling her over his shoulder, he carried her out of the pool.

Side of the pool or house?

"What the hell are you doing?" she asked, pummeling his back.

The house. The privacy was what he needed to give this woman a stern talking to.

"You can't just pick me up and carry me where you want me!" She shouted the words, growling out as she did.

"I'm doing exactly that, baby." He opened the door, closing it gently before going into the sitting room. Ripper placed her on her feet, trapping her hands together inside one of his. "Now, you're going to be punished for what you just said. I don't give a fuck if you like it or not. You go over my fucking knee now and I'll give you five with my hands, or you fight me and I won't let you come for a fucking week. What's it going to be?"

Her arms were folded, but he saw his words had gotten through to her. It was up to Judi how much she wanted to orgasm in the coming week. He knew how talented he was with his tongue. In the past few hours he'd given her more pleasure than she had in her adult life.

"Think before you open those pretty cock sucking lips, baby."

"You're a real bastard."

"You're right about that. I didn't know who my

fucking daddy was."

She growled in frustration once again, stamping her foot. "Fine, I'll go over your knee."

He chuckled at how damn cute she looked losing her temper. The stamping of her foot made her tits bounce in ways that had him thinking of her riding his cock. She really had no idea how fuckable she looked with her flushed skin and bad attitude.

"Get on over." He tapped his knee feeling the excitement building once again. Slowly, she moved over his knees. His tits hung off one side with her stomach in between his thighs. "I'm going to need you to count for me, baby."

"Fuck you."

"And for that bad language we're going to do it without the panties rather than over them." Tugging down the fabric he saw her cream soaking through her pussy lips. The scent was amazing and sweet. Running a finger through her arousal, he sucked the digit into his mouth tasting her. "You're turned on considering you don't want this."

She stayed quiet.

Running his hands over her plump cheeks, he waited until he was ready, and in quick succession landed five even swats against her buttocks. He made sure to keep his hand loose. Ripper wasn't going to hurt her, and he knew with the right pressure he could have bruised her ass up real good for the next week, making it hard for her to sit down.

Once he was done, he sat her on his knee, capturing her jaw so she couldn't look anywhere but at him. "I want to get something clear so you don't go thinking the wrong kind of shit. Devil is never going to cheat on Lexie. Men who are fucking weak and can't keep their dick in their pants cheat. Weak little shits who don't give a fuck about anyone but themselves cheat. Devil is no fucking cheater. He loves that woman and will die protecting her. She has his mark, carries his baby, rides on the back of his bike, and will only ever ride one dick."

Judi tried to pull away from him, but he held onto her. He would not allow her to run from this.

"I will never fucking cheat on you, Judi." With his free hand, he placed it over her pussy. "This is mine, and my dick is yours. I will not cheat on you." No other woman appealed to him, and if they did, he wouldn't go with them. Judi was his woman.

Well, shit. Ripper paused, staring into her eyes as he tried to get his own emotions in order. He didn't promise bitches anything other than a good time.

Why the fuck are you doing it to Judi?

Ignoring the thoughts, he kept hold of her chin as he let his words sink in and righted his own thoughts.

"Men cheat," she said, lips wobbling.

"Weak men cheat. Not me, not us. When we take a woman, we take a woman. There's a difference. If we're with a woman and no promises have been made, then it's free game. You've got my promise, baby. I'm yours. My dick is yours. No one else will get near it."

She nodded, and he watched her bat away the tears.

"Are we clear?"

"Yes, perfectly clear."

"Good, give me those fucking lips as a thank you."

She leaned down, brushing her lips to his. He slid a finger in the slit of her pussy feeling how wet she was. Gripping the back of her head, he held her in place as he fucked her with his digits, stretching her. His cock was in desperate need to fuck. Breaking away from the kiss, he saw her cheeks were a deeper shade of red. "Do you want to go back to the pool?" he asked.

"No."

"What do you want to do?" He waited as she ran a finger down his chest. She traced over the lines of his ink, making him wait.

"I think we should go upstairs and see where this leads," she said, biting her lip.

"Is my princess asking me to take her and fuck her?" he asked, licking the cream from his fingers.

Judi stayed silent, watching him.

"I'm not going anywhere until you say it, baby."

"Why are you making me say it?"

"I like to know the woman I'm about to fuck is there all the way with me. I'm not big on rape, babe. I like to hear that my woman wants my dick as much as I want to give it to her."

She breathed out a sigh. Her nipples had hardened at his words. "I'm never going to get used to the way you talk," she said.

"I'll keep talking to make it better for you." He kissed her lips, waiting.

"Ripper … will you please take me upstairs and fuck me until I'm screaming your name?"

"Baby, nothing would give me greater pleasure."

Standing up, he lifted her over his shoulder like a caveman and carried her upstairs.

"I can walk."

"You've got to reserve your strength."

"This is insane. You're insane."

"I've been insulted with far worse a words," he said, opening her door. This time he left it open as he flipped her to the bed. She did a little bounce before she settled. He stared down at her. The panties were around her knees. In one quick move he had them completely off leaving her in only her bra. "Take it off. Show me those fantastic tits."

"Can you not be so crude?"

"You love it. Your pussy is fucking dripping at my talk." He wasn't going to change for her.

Ripper talked dirty, and he fucked even dirtier. She was just going to have to get used to the way he did things.

She reached behind her back untying the knots holding the bikini bra together. He stared at her tight red nipples as they were exposed to his gaze. His cock hurt from the blood pulsing through it.

"Fuck, baby."

He circled one of her hard nipples before going to the next. She cried out.

"Take my pants off," he said.

Judi moved to the edge of the bed. Her fingers gripped the waistband and slowly lowered them over his rock hard cock. For a split second he closed his eyes at the freedom of being released from the tight underwear.

Opening his eyes, he glanced down to see her looking at his shaft. His foreskin was pulled back showing the enlarged tip, which was glistening from his pre-cum. "Do you want to taste me?" he asked.

She nodded. The movement was so slight that he only just caught it. Stroking her hair, he stepped closer. "Go on then, take me in your mouth."

Her hair was silky soft to the touch. Fingering the length, he watched her lean forward, and in the next breath her tongue poked out to glide over his cream.

Fuck, her tongue felt so good, and she hadn't even taken all of him. Licking his lips, he waited for her to take more. Ripper wasn't going to rush her. After everything she'd been through he was going to let her become acquainted with his cock before he took over, fucking her hard and deep.

"That's it, baby, take me into your mouth."

With both hands he caressed her hair, using every ounce of strength not to ram himself deep into her mouth.

She mumbled, licking along the edge but not taking him deep.

Come on, Princess, my sanity will only last so long.

He didn't go any deeper, letting Judi set the pace.
****

The salty taste of Ripper's pre-cum exploded on her tongue. Judi was so surprised by the lust that gripped her, and she felt the inner walls of her pussy clench in response. She held onto his legs as she moved her tongue along the side of the pulsing vein. His fingers caressed her hair but didn't hold her head to force his way into her mouth. Each movement calmed her nerves until she was confident enough to take the tip into her mouth.

"Holy fuck, have mercy," he said.

She didn't believe he was talking to her. It would take some getting used to his language, but he didn't lie. His words did arouse her in ways she didn't think was possible. Judi took another inch of him into her mouth, sucking tightly and flicking the tip with her tongue to swallow more of his cum.

"I wasn't wrong. Your lips are made for sucking cock, my cock."

Humming in agreement, she sank her nails into his flesh as she went as deep as his cock would go. When he hit the back of her throat she drew up, giving herself a few seconds before sliding back down. She'd perfected the art of sucking cock without it hurting, but some men were not patient.

Forget about them. Only Ripper.

His hands gripped her hair tightly making it burn

where he held her. She moaned as the pain went straight to her pussy.

"That's it, baby. Take your time. Love my cock. No one is in any rush to come."

One of his hands left her hair to reach down and stroke her breasts. His hands were so large he cupped one breast easily. "I'm going to fuck these tits, baby."

She listened to him talking as she took him to the back of her throat. The moment she was about to gag she released him.

"I'm going to get you to hold these tits together as I slide between them. When I come I'll coat them with my cum. You'll look so fucking sexy decorated with my cum," he said.

Gripping the base of his shaft, she took him as deep as she could. This time she couldn't stop the gag reflex.

Ripper pulled away instantly, stepping out of reach. "I love your mouth on me, Judi. Don't hurt yourself. I'm not a customer. I'm here because I want to be, and I want your pleasure as much as I want your own."

Judi felt like crying. His words touched her deeply.

"Okay."

He stepped closer, and she took him back into her mouth, caressing his balls as she sucked his cock. She'd never liked giving oral, but Ripper tasted fresh and clean. His hands and words soothed her every second that passed.

After several minutes he tugged on her hair, pulling her off. "It's time I tasted your sweet pussy."

She went to protest, but he sank to his knees, opening her legs wide. Sitting on the edge of the bed she watched him open her lips exposing her to him.

"So fucking pretty," he said.

His lips soon replaced his fingers driving her closer to orgasm.

Collapsing to the bed she felt his tongue flick over her clit. He slid down, fucking her with several hard strokes before going to circle her clit.

Within minutes of him licking her, she felt her orgasm close to the surface. Whimpering, she thrashed on the bed.

"No, I'm not going to let you come until I'm inside you." Ripper stood up, wiping her juices from his chin.

"Please," she said, begging.

"You can beg me all you want. I'm not going to give in. If you don't want my cock inside you then I'll lick you, but I will be sleeping in another room. I don't know how much I can stand if you don't want to fuck."

Judi went to her elbows looking at him. "You're telling me you won't sleep with me for fear of not being able to listen to me say no?"

"Yeah. You're going to have to realize you're fucking sexy." He gripped his cock, working the length from root to tip. "I want to fuck you, Judi. I should be fucking killed for what I want to do to you."

She bit her lip, not knowing what to say.

It's sweet.

Sweet and Ripper didn't really go in the same sentence.

"I want you to fuck me, Ripper. I don't know about afterwards."

"Get into the center of the bed," he said, ordering her.

Judi moved to the middle looking up at the ceiling. The bed dipped under his weight as he crawled toward her. He didn't climb over her or ram on home.

Ripper settled beside her, holding onto her stomach.

"Calm down, baby. We're having fun here."

She didn't even know she'd tensed up at his closeness.

Turning to him, she stared into his green eyes and let the love she'd developed for him take over. She cupped his cheek feeling the stubble of the day's growth. There were many times over the last two years when he felt untouchable to her. If she touched him, he'd disappear.

So many times during Rob's ownership she had imagined a knight coming to her rescue. She'd been so naive and stupid thinking someone was going to come to *her* rescue. In all of her fantasies not once were any of the men wearing leather or riding bikes. Ripper was a killer, he lived by the club's code, not by the normal code, and yet, like Devil, he was her savior.

"I'm right here, Ripper. I'm right where I want to be."

His hand cupped her cheek with his thumb caressing over her bottom lip. "You're something else. You really don't know how fucking special you are."

He broke the distance, claiming her lips. She moaned, opening up to his searching tongue. Ripper took his time, loving her mouth before kissing his way to her neck. Whimpering, she turned her head so he got better access to kiss her.

"That's it, baby. Kiss me back. Open up to me."

Running her hands down his back, a yearning started back up. The kissing and touching were not enough.

"Please, Ripper."

"Are you ready for me?" he asked.

She nodded.

The bed dipped again, and she watched him

grabbing a condom from the desk in the corner. "I left it here earlier."

"You don't have to use one," she said.

"Are you on the pill?" he asked.

Judi nodded. She was on a low dosage pill to help control her monthly cycle. The doctor did warn her that it couldn't be guaranteed as a contraceptive, but it did work.

"I'm still going to use this the first time."

He tore into the foil and placed the latex over his cock. His cock was long and thick. She was surprised a condom actually fit over the length of him.

When he came back to her, she lay back gazing at him. This time he didn't go to her side but rested between her legs. She opened wide enough for him.

His fingers skimmed up the outside of her legs then back down.

"Look at me, Judi."

She returned her gaze to his.

"Who am I?"

"Ripper."

"Who do you feel safe with?"

"You." She answered him without difficulty.

"Do you want this?"

Smiling, she nodded. "Yes."

"Then eyes on me at all times."

She could only nod her head again. He reached down gripping his shaft.

Glancing down she saw him sliding the covered tip through her slit. The moment he bumped her clit she cried out at the pleasure exploding inside her.

"So fucking swollen. You want to be fucked," he said.

Judi couldn't argue. Her body was on fire with the need for his cock.

He didn't plunge inside her. Ripper glided through her slit to her entrance. He pressed so she opened up to the head. When she took the head, he withdrew going to her clit to slide over the nub.

Over and over he did this making her ache with need to feel him stretching inside her.

"Please, Ripper, fuck me," she said, screaming out the words.

"Do you want my cock?" he asked.

"Yes."

Gripping his hands, she sank her nails into his flesh hoping he would get the message about how desperately she wanted him.

He didn't let up, torturing her by holding back his cock. Flinging back to the bed, she cried out in frustration. Ripper must have been satisfied with how desperate she was. He slid the tip to her entrance, and in one thrust of his hips, he slammed deep inside her.

Sheer heaven.

Chapter Nine

Judi's pussy was tight as fuck. Ripper moved his hands up to grip hers beside her head. He held her tightly, staring into her eyes, which had grown wide at his penetration. Her pussy was far more pleasurable than her mouth. Fuck, he needed to stay still just so he didn't blow his load straight away.

Fuck, shit, cunt.

The words ran through his mind as he tried to get his bearings over what was happening. None of this felt real to him, and yet it was completely real. His feelings for Judi couldn't be mistaken. He'd always cared about her, but those feelings were fucking hard to ignore now. With the feel of her cunt wrapped around his cock, his heart pounded, and there was no getting away from the love he felt for her.

For years he'd screwed his way through women, none of them meaning anything to him at all until Judi.

She made him want to feel shit.

"Are you okay?" he asked, staring into her brown eyes.

"Yes, I'm fine."

"You're fine with my dick inside you?" Ripper pretended to be insulted, sliding a little deeper inside her.

Judi gasped, arching up to him.

"Do you feel me now? It's more than fine."

Her moans took over, and he held her in place. Ripper felt every ripple of her pussy. The pulse at her throat was pounding against her skin. Leaning down he sucked on her pulse feeling her whimper at his touch. "Tell me what's going through your head?"

"You're so big. There's nothing else I can feel besides you inside me." She bit her lip as he kissed her neck, nibbling on bits of flesh.

"I'm going to fuck you in a minute."

She gasped, and he felt her pussy tighten around him. Without the condom he imagined he would feel every drop of her cum. He wished there wasn't a layer of protection between them. Her fingers tightened around his hands, holding onto him tightly.

"Please, Ripper," she said.

"What do you want, baby?"

Claiming her lips, he stopped her from voicing her need. This time her tongue peeked out looking to meet with his. He gave as good as he got, slamming his tongue deep into her mouth. Ripper wanted to possess, to own, and to show to her with his cock whom she belonged to.

"I want you to fuck me."

"I am fucking you." He leaned down, kissing her neck and smiled.

She growled. "Move!"

"You're not enjoying what I'm doing?"

"Yes, please, fuck me," she said, begging him.

He moved out of her tight heat 'til only the tip of his cock was inside her. She cried out, whimpering. Staring down at where they were joined, Ripper almost lost it. His condom covered cock was slick from her cream. "Look at us, baby. Look at how fucking perfect your pussy is."

He growled the last word as he fucked her hard, slamming back to the hilt inside her. She cried out.

Releasing her hands, he grabbed her hips and fucked her hard and fast. She held onto his shoulder, her nails gripping his flesh. Ripper felt the sting of her touch, but he loved it. He'd gladly wear her mark for the rest of his life.

"Look at us, baby. Look at us fucking." He'd intended to take their first time slowly. There was no chance of that. Her tight heat made it impossible for him to focus on anything. She looked between them crying out as he fucked her hard. "Put your hands flat to the headboard."

He waited for her to do as he asked.

With her palms flat against the board, he gripped her hips and rammed home. Each thrust inside her pussy had her moving up against the bed. The hold on the bed stopped her from hitting her head.

The feel of her tight pussy was driving him crazy.

Reaching down he flicked her clit. He watched her orgasm as well as felt the tightness of her cunt. She screamed out, driving down onto his cock.

"So fucking tight. I'm going to fuck you all night long. You're not going to be able to walk for a fucking week when I'm done with you." Harder he plunged inside her, driving deeper.

He felt her cervix from the depth of his penetration.

"Please, fuck, please," she said, screaming.

"That's it, baby. Orgasm for me. Let me feel your tight cunt." Her tits bounced from the force of his thrusts. He watched them, loving the tightness of her red buds.

"Ripper, please."

"I want you to come for me, baby. Give me your cum." He felt his own release close to the surface. Gritting his teeth he waited for her to reach her second release. When she did, he fucked her harder and longer until the first stirrings began.

Together they cried out, and he dug his fingers into her hips, tight. Ripper knew his fingerprints would be marked on her skin. She would have to keep them covered from Devil and Lexie. If it was up to him, he'd get her to show them off. Judi was his woman, and he had every intention of keeping her.

The love he felt was no longer going to be ignored or denied.

He placed his hands either side of her head, looking down at her. Shaken to the core, he saw tears were blooming in her eyes.

"I never knew it could be like that," she said.

"It can get a whole lot better."

Leaning down, he placed a kiss on her lips wanting to do a hell of a lot more. He held back, giving Judi more space to move.

Something had shifted between them.

"I don't know how it can get better," she said, licking her lips.

"This is our first time." He was testing the waters to see how far she can go. The last thing he wanted to do was leave her feeling scared or thinking about her past.

"I'm going to pull out and take care of the condom. Will you be okay?"

She nodded. The motion was a simple jerk of the head. Cupping the back of her neck, he slammed his lips down on hers.

"I'm not going anywhere, baby. There is more to come."

Her smile caught at his heart. Shit, he was starting to feel like a fucking pussy.

"Don't let them in." Ripper touched her temple trying to force the bad memories away.

Climbing out of her tight heat, he walked into the bedroom to deal with the used condom.

Washing his dick, he wiped himself clean before going back in the bedroom. She had moved under the covers and was looking up at the ceiling. Her gaze landed on him when he walked into the bedroom. Checking the clock, he saw it was only a little after nine.

"I'm not sitting in bed waiting for sleep. Come

on." He pushed the blanket away, picking her up in his arms and headed back downstairs.

"Will you stop doing this? I can walk."

"I know you can walk, but you'll fight me. We've fucked, and you're doing whatever female shit you're doing. We're going to watch a movie or do something fun." Turning into the sitting room, he dropped her down onto the sofa.

"I'm naked, Ripper."

"So am I." He turned the switch on and started going up and down the channels. Grabbing the remote, he settled behind Judi, cupping a breast as he looked for something to watch.

"I'm tired."

"No, you're not." He found a horror movie and left it playing. Stroking the curve of her nipple, he felt his arousal start to build.

Judi didn't say anything as he played with her body. She was so fucking responsive. Her tits were one of her best features. He was looking forward to watching those tits bounce in front of his face.

"I hate horror movies," she said.

"I could put the porn channel on if you'd prefer."

She giggled. "You watch porn?"

"Every man watches porn. I prefer to watch real life shit than the crap they're always shoving in our faces. There is nothing attractive about a woman being spit on." Judi had turned her head to look at him. She wrinkled her nose at his description.

"That's gross."

"It's business, and it's shit. I for one can't stand it, but it gets the rocks off when needed." He'd not watched porn for years.

"I think you're trying to shock me," she said, turning back to face the television.

"I'm not. Sex should be wet and dirty." He leaned down sliding a finger between her slit. "Your pussy is wet and can take a good hard cock. If you were dry I couldn't fuck you."

He plunged two fingers inside her wet warmth. She felt soft to the touch.

Biting the side of her neck, he sucked on the flesh being careful not to mark her. Devil would start asking questions, and until she was ready he wasn't going to force the issue.

****

The following morning Judi woke up to Ripper's arms wrapped around her. Last night's conversation about porn movies brought a sudden flush to her skin. The horror movie ended up being forgotten as Ripper bent her over and fucked her from behind. He had cupped her breasts until there were fingerprint bruises around her flesh as he pounded away inside her. His passion surprised her. He brought her to orgasm multiple times.

She'd gone from never having experienced an orgasm to being forced to have multiple.

Staring at the clock she saw it was past ten o'clock. Groaning, she dropped her head to the side of the bed.

"What's the matter, baby?" he asked, startling her.

"How long have you been awake?" She glanced behind her to see his eyes open, staring at her.

"Long enough. You snore, you know, and mutter shit in your sleep."

"You know I don't have a clue about your name," she said. Judi didn't know half of the Chaos Bleeds' real names. She liked their road names. Ripper suited him for some reason.

"It's Daniel Hill, but I won't respond to that name. I've been Ripper for a long time." He rubbed a hand down his face, glancing over to look at the clock. "No wonder I'm fucking starving."

She chuckled. "I'll make you some food, Daniel."

His hand tightened around her waist. "Oh no, you don't. You're not going anywhere." Ripper gripped her waist hauling her up to straddle his waist. She squealed, giggling as she felt the evidence of his arousal between her thighs.

"Don't you ever get tired?" she asked, moaning.

Ripper cupped her breasts then pinched her nipples. Crying out, she pressed her chest toward his touch.

"If I touch your pussy will you be wet?"

She looked down into his eyes. "I don't know."

He slapped her ass, making her burn. "Don't lie to me."

"Yes, I'm wet."

"And you're complaining about my need? I need to get some fucking pills to keep up with you. My dick will only get hard so much."

Judi rolled her eyes, chuckling at his words. "You're more than capable of keeping up, baby."

She leaned down, feeling his hands move down to her hips. The endearment felt natural when speaking to him. Cupping his face, she claimed his lips, caressing the flesh with her tongue. He opened up inviting her inside.

"Kiss me back," he said.

She did, loving his lips with her own.

Ripper tore away from her first, lifting her up to slide down on his cock. She was sore from their fucking last night, but this was different. He took his time, sliding inside her slowly.

A moan broke through her lips. Her need gripped

her and took her by surprise.

"So fucking tight. This is my pussy, Judi. No other man is allowed near this body."

"I know. It will only ever belong to you." She couldn't take the words back.

"Who do you belong to?"

"You, Ripper, you."

"Good girl." He cupped her ass, drawing her down then up on his shaft. Crying out, she held onto his rock hard abs as she fucked him. "I knew it. I knew your tits would look so fucking perfect swinging above me."

She got a buzz knowing he'd been thinking about her. Opening her eyes, she stared down into his. The lust blazed back at her threatening to scorch her. There was no other place for her to go.

Holding onto his abs, sliding up and down his cock, there was nowhere else she wanted to go. Ripper made her yearn for him.

"You're mine now, Judi. Never letting you fucking go."

Judi closed her eyes as the pleasure took over. His cock was hard inside her, pushing against her cervix. The depth of his cock was on the verge of pain. The two combinations were a match made in heaven. Her body came alive as he fucked her harder.

"Touch your clit, baby. Come all over my cock."

Reaching down, she stroked her clit gasping as the tiniest stroke took her over the edge. Her body was no longer her own but Ripper's to do with as he pleased.

"Fuck, so fucking perfect." His hands went to her hips, and he pounded away inside her, going deeper than ever before.

They cried out together as Ripper went over the edge. When they were done, she wiped the sweat from her brow, chuckling. "Now that's the best way to start the morning," she said, kissing his lips.

His hands banded around her, grounding her tumultuous emotions. She felt safe in his arms, like nothing was ever going to bother her with him close by.

"I meant what I said."

Glancing up, she saw he had pushed a pillow underneath his head.

"About what?" She tucked some hair behind her ears.

"You're mine. No man goes near you at all. No dates, no flirting, nothing."

She smiled. "Ripper, I don't date, and I rarely go out. Lexie and Phoebe are my friends, no one else." For fun she babysat for the two women. Yeah, her world was full of excitement.

"You're something else, Judi. Any man would give his right arm to have you by his side."

"I'm not like that." She felt uncomfortable. Had he forgotten she used to sell her body for money?

He gripped her chin, forcing her to look at him. "Your body is your own. That fucking bastard forced you to sell yourself. Stop thinking about that shit like it's all you are. It's not."

She went to open her lips when she heard the door open.

Eyes opening wide, she stared at Ripper as she listened.

"Come on, kids, I'm hungry," Devil said.

"Shit, Devil's home." Panic descended on her.

Being caught naked with Ripper deeply inside her was not going to go well at all. Scrambling off his cock, she winced at the sudden pain from the width of him. She wasn't used to having a rock hard cock between her thighs.

"Judi, are you home?" Lexie asked, shouting

upstairs.

"Yeah, I'm here." She shouted the words, hoping Lexie would stay downstairs.

"We heard Ripper is staying with you. Where is he?"

Pulling up her shorts, she saw Ripper had the sense to bring his clothes with him. "Answer her," Ripper said, whispering.

Her hands were shaking like mad. Crap, this was not what she wanted.

Judi put a shirt over her head, forgetting about the bra as she jumped up on the bed starting to gather her stuff.

"Erm," she said, speaking.

Shit, what was she supposed to say?

Her door suddenly opened, and Lexie appeared. Screaming out, she grabbed an armful of the blanket. Thinking fast, she stared at the floor.

"It's there, Ripper. It's big and ugly." Screaming, she tried to get her nerves under control. She'd never been capable of lying.

He looked at her frowning.

Come on, play the fuck along.

"What's going on?" Lexie asked, opening the door. She looked from Ripper to Judi then back again. The suspicion was clear on her face.

"I'm telling you it's the size of a tarantula. I saw it coming out of the bathroom. Please kill it for me." Judi let the words run out.

"A spider, I'm here to kill a spider."

Lexie screamed, diving onto the bed. "Spiders, I hate spiders. Devil!" She shouted his name in desperation.

Great thinking, Judi.

Seconds later Devil was running into the room

carrying a baby spoon. "What? What the fuck is it?"

"A spider. Judi saw a spider."

The two women held each other. Glancing at Ripper, she saw him roll his eyes.

She did her best not to respond. How else was she going to explain Ripper being in her room?

"What the fuck you doing in her room?" Devil asked.

"Looking for a spider apparently. Your girl is a fucking wimp." Ripper looked around the floor.

Now the problem was actually finding a spider for him to kill.

"Are you sure you saw anything?" Devil asked.

"Please, don't let a spider be walking around the house, Devil. I'm in a delicate condition." Lexie rubbed her stomach.

Judi noticed the color was back in her cheeks. "Did you have fun?" she asked.

"Yeah, we couldn't stay though. The smells of breakfast were too much. Some people actually ordered fish," Lexie said, shuddering.

Devil started laughing. "She insulted the whole spa by throwing up over the table. Lex demanded I leave and cut our trip short."

Laughing, Judi glanced over at Ripper. In the next couple of minutes he pretended to catch the spider and throw it out.

Lexie finally left the bed with Devil's arms wrapped around her.

"A spider?" Ripper asked, kissing the top of her head when they were alone.

"I panicked."

Everyone was afraid of spiders, even her. She was more afraid of what Devil would do the moment he realized she was fucking Ripper.

****

Later that day Devil sat behind his desk at his home thinking about what Tiny had just said. Zero had told the club everything. Alan hadn't struck yet apart from the nurse, but his friend knew it was only a matter of time before Alan hit out again. Lexie stood by the doorframe, folding her arms over her chest.

"What are you thinking?" she asked.

"I've got a feeling shit is going to hit the fan," he said. He never kept anything from her. She gave him everything, and in return he told her the truth.

He watched her walk toward him. She leaned against the desk staring down at him. Reaching out, he pulled her close, kissing her stomach. After the last few weeks of arguing she'd finally convinced him there was nothing wrong but morning sickness.

Her fingers sank into his hair.

"What has actually happened?"

"One of Zero's friends turned up at the clubhouse with a bullet wound to her stomach. She's fine, but this guy is causing a lot of trouble. He's taken out a nurse that fucked Zero, and they're on lockdown. Tiny is keeping me updated, but none of the others know. He's worried," Devil said, kissing her stomach. "Zero did something in his past, and he fucked up. He's paying the price for his mistake."

"Is this like Snitch?"

He shook his head. "No, he wanted vengeance. This is a death sentence for Zero. Someone wants him dead, but they want him to suffer first. I've got a feeling this is going to end up a nightmare for The Skulls."

Devil loved the feel of her fingers in his hair, holding onto him.

"Will you go if they ask for help?"

"I've got to, baby. Tiny is a friend." She smiled,

but he saw the fear in her eyes. Cupping her cheek, he stood up staring down into her eyes. "You're my entire fucking world. I will never do anything that will put us at risk."

"I know the club means so much to you."

"Hey." He held onto her face stopping her from looking away. "The club is my life, but you're my reason for fucking living. I love you, baby. I'm not going anywhere." Devil kissed her lips. "If I know it's a death mission, me and the boys will bail. It's not my fight, and you and my boys come first."

Devil wouldn't do anything to hurt her. He wanted to see his baby born and spend the rest of his years growing old with his woman.

Holding her close he thought about Ripper this morning. The way the other man had looked at Judi had Devil's gut tightening.

Something was going on between the couple. He didn't know what it was. Devil only hoped Ripper had his head on straight. Judi was off limits, and he wasn't going to budge on this.

Chapter Ten

The following week Ripper was doing everything to avoid being alone with Devil. The biggest mistake he could make was thinking Devil didn't see everything. There was a reason he was named after the ruler of hell. Their president saw everything. Shit, he was making himself feel nervous.

Looking over his bike he started to make sure there were no faults. Devil was inside the clubhouse going over the books that Vincent brought with him from the strip club. The strip club was doing better business than the mechanic shop. Some of the rich folk didn't like bikers working on their expensive cars.

Ripper didn't care. He loved working with his hands at every opportunity.

Once he was sure his bike was in the best condition he started to give it a clean, working over the body of the machine. Sweat dotted his back, and it was taking all of his strength not to text Judi. The last time they'd been together was three days ago when he convinced her to go for a ride with him late at night. She was staying around, studying for the most part.

He couldn't keep stopping by the house as otherwise Devil would think he had a thing for Lexie. In the last couple of weeks he'd come to see it had nothing to do with Lexie. All he'd wanted from her was a fuck. She was a sweet woman, sexy as hell and one fine dancer. Most guys would want to fuck her.

She was taken, and his thoughts were dominated by Judi.

Curse stood over him causing a shadow. The other man was one of his closest friends. "Ashley told me to send you out a coffee," he said, holding a cup.

"Are you a waitress now?" Ripper asked,

standing up.

"She was bouncing on my dick ten minutes ago. I need the break."

"I'm surprised you're not at the diner in town lusting after sweet, dark-haired Mia." Ripper teased his friend. They had both been to the diner, and each time Curse barely said a word to the waitress even though he couldn't tear his eyes away from her.

"Why are you avoiding Devil?" Curse asked.

The smile dropped before he could stop. Shit, he thought he'd been doing well to avoid Devil without being noticeable.

"I'm not."

"Liar. You've turned up late to every meeting about The Skulls. You're always out working, and you just happen to need to leave when he turns up. What's going on?" Curse asked, folding his arms.

"Nothing." An image of Judi riding his cock entered his mind.

Shit, get it under control.

"You're lying. Devil wants you inside anyway."

Panic struck him instantly. Wiping his hands on the grease cloth, he gave Curse back the empty cup. Without saying another word he walked toward the clubhouse. Several men and women were cleaning, drinking, and generally having a good time. He saw Pussy trying to convince Ashley to a dirty dance.

Going straight to Devil's office, he knocked and entered. The door was already open.

"Come in, sit down," Devil said, looking over a file on his desk.

"What can I do for you?" Ripper asked, wiping his hands, which had gone sweaty the moment he entered the office.

"Just a minute." Devil ticked something down on

the file and looked up. "Why are you avoiding me?"

"I'm not. I'm standing right here."

"Don't wise ass me, Ripper. We all agreed to settle down in Piston County. I can't run this club if any of my boys are keeping shit from me."

On the road, Devil demanded respect and for him to know everything from the smallest dispute to the biggest business deal.

"Nothing is wrong."

"Is there anything going on between you and Judi? I noticed the looks going on. I'm not a fucking idiot."

Tell him. Let the truth be aired. This is your opportunity.

"Nothing is going on. I was helping Judi out. She doesn't always feel comfortable in her own skin. That morning she found a spider." He rolled his eyes opening his arms to show he didn't care. "Women, I'll never understand them."

"Why haven't you been around the club?"

"I've needed fresh air. I drive my bike up to the picnic area to overlook the town. It fills the need." The lies were pouring out, and Ripper hated them. It would be a lot easier for him to come out with the truth, but Judi wasn't ready for Devil to know.

So many people had lost her respect by not listening to her. He wasn't going to be one of those people.

"Are you regretting settling down? I can find a spot for you in another club if you're wanting to go back to the road," Devil said.

"No, this is where I'm going to stay. What's happening with Zero? I know shit is hitting the fan for him." Ripper tried to change the subject diverting Devil's attention.

For the next couple of minutes he was brought up to speed with everything that was going on in Fort Wills. There was nothing new to report. Zero was still trying to find out about Alan's whereabouts, but he was keeping a protective vigil over the woman who was shot as well as the rest of the club.

"When we're called to help, do you want to come?" Devil asked.

"Do you really think it's going to come to that?"

"Yeah. When a woman is shot it's not long after when trouble starts." Devil shrugged. "What do you want to do?"

"I'll stay behind and keep an eye on the women and the business." He couldn't leave Judi behind. The very thought had him breaking out into a sweat.

"Fair enough. Some of the boys want to go on the road. I'll give them a shot while you stay here." Devil nodded at him, dismissing him.

Getting up, he went back to his bike to clean it. Later that day Lexie and Judi turned her. He felt her gaze on him, and he forced himself to keep cleaning the other bikes beside his.

Ashley ran out, jumping into his arms. The sun was beating down on him. He wrapped his arms around Ashley, using the moment to look at Judi. The moment he did, he wished he hadn't. She looked like she'd been kicked in the gut. With Elizabeth on her hip she followed Lexie inside the clubhouse.

"Some of us are going to the strip club tonight. Are you in?" Ashley asked.

"Is Curse going?"

"Yeah, it's his idea. I'm going, but I'm not dancing or anything. Pussy and Death are also going." Ashley was a bubbly woman. She always found something to smile about. Some of the other sweet-butts despised her. Ripper actually liked her. From the look of pain in Judi's eyes, he wished he hadn't fucked her.

He couldn't lie to her, and he got a feeling when they were alone she would ask him.

"I'm going to go and tell Curse," Ashley said, jumping up and down.

"Tell me what?" The man appeared beside her.

"Ripper's coming to the club as well."

Smiling, he looked toward the clubhouse wondering what was going on inside.

"Lexie's showing off her latest ultrasound picture. The doctor has also confirmed she had morning sickness. She'll be all right with a good diet and rest. Judi's sticking beside her like glue," Curse said. "He's got a bit of a thing for Lex." Curse spoke to Ashley.

"No, I don't." Ripper disputed his feelings.

Neither of them listened.

An hour later he entered the clubhouse finding Judi sitting in the corner with Elizabeth and Simon. She ignored him as he made his way upstairs to get changed.

On the way down, he saw she was getting ready to leave with Lexie and Devil.

"Where are you going?" Devil asked, before he could leave.

"Some of us are headed to the strip club," Curse said, speaking up. "We're going to party in style. It could be one of our last times."

Glancing toward Judi he saw the very thought had her upset.

"I'm going to wait in the car." She held Simon's hand as she walked out of the clubhouse not even looking his way.

He felt Devil's gaze on him. Shit, he needed to keep his thoughts to himself. Following Curse out of the clubhouse, he waited for Ashley to get on the back of

Curse's bike before riding toward the strip club.

It was too early to be open to the public. Curse had a key as he was looking after the building for Vincent. They all took turns manning the place for the club.

Inside the club he saw the women practicing for their turn on stage. He sat in the corner as some of the men went to the bar or behind to see the women. Ripper sat back, resting his head against the wall.

Judi's pain-filled face entered his thoughts.

Don't feel guilty.

She's mine.

Bouncing his knee he looked around the club knowing he didn't really want to be here but with her. She'd really invaded his fucking life and made him fall in love with her.

There, it was out for him to finally accept.

****

Eating the potato salad, Judi couldn't taste it. Her thoughts were on Ripper with Ashley. She hated how relaxed the woman was with him. Watching her fling herself in Ripper's arms and him catching her, cut Judi deeply. She'd not trusted anyone to hold her in such a long time.

Men cheat.

Devil doesn't cheat.

"How's college going?" Devil asked, invading her troubled thoughts.

"It's going good." She forced a smile to her lips when she looked at him. There was nothing else she could think to say. Lexie was watching her along with Devil. "How is everything going at the club?"

"It's good. We may have to leave if things go bad for The Skulls."

She nodded. Judi liked The Skulls. She really

liked Angel. The other woman was so sweet. The first time she met Angel she'd been taken by surprise. No woman who was married to a biker should have that air of innocence, yet Angel still did.

"The Skulls are good people. I hope nothing bad happens to them." She thought about the man she shot well over two weeks ago. Her stomach turned remembering the whole incident.

"You're not feeling ill are you, honey? You're not eating anything," Lexie said, pointing at the plate in front of her.

"I'm fine. I'm just not hungry." She placed her fork down, smiling at her family. "Everything is fine though."

They looked at her doubtfully.

"Ripper is staying behind in case anything happens," Devil said, speaking up.

"I'm sure he likes that," Judi said, glancing down at her wrists. From their first time she still had the bruises on her hips and breasts. She made sure to wear long shirts so none of the bruises were seen.

"Is there something going on between the two of you?" Devil asked.

She shook her head. "No, I'm going to start the dishes." Grabbing her plate along with a couple of empty bowls she headed toward the kitchen. Throwing her food into the bin, she rinsed the plate before placing it in the dishwasher.

Seconds later she heard Lexie clear her throat. Turning around, she saw her friend looked a little worried. "Is there anything you want to talk about?" she asked.

"Did Devil send you in?"

"No. He's thinking about Tiny and what's going on in Fort Wills."

"You've got him to stop worrying about you and the baby." Judi worked to clean the plates and dishes, loading them into the dishwasher.

"Don't change the subject. I know there're only a few years between us, but I worry about you, Judi." The concern was easy to hear in her voice.

"There's nothing to worry about at all. I promise I'm fine."

"You look hurt."

Turning toward her friend she smiled at Lexie. "I'm not hurt. I'm tired. It has been a long couple of days, and the heat is making my head hurt. I think I stayed outside too long." She wiped her hands on a towel. Going to Lexie, she wrapped her arms around her shoulders. "I promise, nothing is wrong."

"Go get some rest," Lexie said. "We'll have a girly day tomorrow."

Nodding, she made her way up to her bedroom. Closing and locking her door, she sat on the edge of the bed. Tears filled her eyes blurring out the view in front of her.

Wrapping her arms around her shoulders she tried to deal with the pain exploding inside her chest. She couldn't come apart in front of Devil or Lexie. They would all know why she was crying. Wiping her face, she forced herself to take a deep breath and stand up.

Her phone buzzed, and she grabbed it to see a message from Ripper.

With her shoulders slumped, she opened the message even though she didn't want to.

Ripper: What r u doing?

Seriously? Her anger spiking, she sent him back a quick reply.

Judi: Leave me the fuck alone.

Throwing the phone onto the bed she entered the

bathroom, turning on the shower. Glancing at her reflection she shook her head. She was so gullible. The first man to show her any kind of attention and she fell hook, line and sinker.

Turning away, she undressed quickly and took her sweet time in the shower. She loved the hot water cascading over her body.

The time passed as she soaped her skin, the warmth finally heating up her cold bones. When she climbed out, wrapping a towel in her hair she felt much better. Entering her bedroom she came to a stop as Ripper sat on the edge of her bed. His face showed his anger.

Glancing toward her door she saw it was still locked. Turning to the doors overlooking the garden she saw it was open.

"What the hell are you doing?" she asked, folding her arms underneath her breasts. Judi made sure to keep her voice down so the others in the house were not aware of someone in her room.

"You wouldn't answer my texts. I didn't like what you said."

He stared at her then his gaze wandered down her body. From his look alone she felt on fire.

"You shouldn't be here, Ripper. Devil can come at any time."

"They never check on you since he walked in on your naked. He was scared at seeing you without your clothes on," Ripper said, standing up.

She tried to stand her ground. Ripper stepped closer, and she couldn't help but back away.

"Don't come near me."

"I haven't cheated on you."

Judi snorted, taking a step back. She hit the wall, and she growled in annoyance at being stopped from getting away from him. "You've not fucked Ashley then?"

She saw his jaw tense.

"I fucked her before you and I got involved."

"When?" she asked, knowing in her heart she didn't want to know the answer.

He shook his head.

"Tell me."

Ripper caught the knot of her towel and tugged. The towel opened up falling to the floor.

"You really want to know?"

No, I don't, you bastard. I've fallen in love with you, and you're a total bastard and a liar.

She didn't say any of the words that were running around her mind.

"Fine, the last time I fucked her was the day after I buried your first kill. I woke up with you in my arms, and I was fucking horny. I've never been so turned on before, and yet you made me fucking ache to be inside your pussy."

His words took her completely by surprise.

"So you fucked her?"

"I screwed her because I couldn't have you. Do you know how hard it is for me to want you?" he asked. His voice was hard as he spoke. She saw the torment in his eyes, in every single word he spoke. "I saw that animal fucking beating you. I wanted to hurt him, and you were just a fucking girl. I shouldn't be having these thoughts about you, Judi, but I am. What kind of monster does that make me?" he asked, thumping his chest.

Before she could answer, he claimed her lips. This was rough, passion filled, and she could only hold onto him as he took charge. The towel binding her hair on top of her head was tugged away. He fisted the length at the same time as he grabbed a handful of her ass.

She cried out at the bite of pain. Ripper released her hair to press a hand over her mouth. "You've got to be quiet." She was going to go insane if she couldn't speak up.

Nodding her head, she reached between them to unbuckle his belt. This was insane, crazy, and so dangerous. The anger she'd felt minutes before evaporated turning into lust. She eased his cock out, fisting the length.

He growled against her neck, lifting her up.

Circling her legs around his waist she bit into her lip as he sank to the hilt inside her.

"There is no one else but you, baby," he said, whispering the words against her ear. "I don't know how else to tell you that you're the only bitch who exists in my world."

"Don't call me that." She placed her fingers over his mouth. Her hand over his mouth didn't stop him from talking.

"It doesn't matter what I call you, you're still mine. It doesn't make me want you any less than I already do."

She hissed as he slammed to the hilt inside her. His cock scraped along her inner walls. Within minutes her cream soaked over his cock making his penetration easier.

Gasping, she moaned, and Ripper covered her mouth to muffle the sounds of her moans. He held her against the wall, fucking her hard.

There was no hiding her feelings as he fucked her hard, taking over every part of her senses. Ripper owned every inch of her.

"Mine, always fucking mine," he said.

"Yes."

She stared into his eyes. The green depths

captured her making her feel whole from his look alone. Together they found their peak of pleasure going over it. His cock jerked inside her pulsing his cum into her womb.

There was no going back from now on. They were bound together in ways that words could not describe. Ripper had captured her heart and bound her soul to his.

Chapter Eleven

The summer was at its peak, and so far The Skulls were not in danger. Devil was hosting another barbeque, but instead of feeling nervous, Ripper looked forward to it. Any chance he got to be with Judi he took it. Whenever she needed to go into town to the library he would follow her, hanging out with her as she studied. She was the first woman he loved to watch study. He liked the way she bit her lip as she worked through her latest assignment.

Lexie's morning sickness had finally settled down, and she no longer looked pale or sick. Devil had also calmed down with Lexie looking healthy. Grabbing a beer from the cooler Ripper stared around the garden at his fellow brothers along with some of Piston County's wealthy families. Devil's barbeques had become famous among the county, and anybody showed up. He saw one family keep their daughter guarded when Pussy stepped close. Shaking his head, Ripper tried not to laugh at the sight. Anyone would think they were Neanderthal beasts hoping to take and rape their daughters. The thought alone had the smile disappearing from his face.

Taking a long gulp of his drink he spotted Judi moving away from the pool. Ashley was talking to her as they walked. He checked Judi's face to make sure the other woman wasn't upsetting her. When her gaze landed on him, Ripper felt like he was on fire. Fuck, he really did love that woman. Judi had invaded his heart and soul. He would have gone to Devil about his thoughts, but Judi wasn't ready for anyone to know about them.

"I'm going to go look for Curse. I look forward to shopping with you," Ashley said, saying her goodbyes. She smiled at him before looking for Curse.

"Do I even want to know what's going on

between you two?" he asked, keeping his distance. She grabbed a soda from the cooler, rubbing her breasts across his arm as she bent down. Bitch was doing it on purpose if her smile was anything to go by.

"We're not comparing notes if that's what you're worried about," she said, smiling.

"You're going to be the death of me."

They stood together looking out over the garden. Lexie was smiling as Devil talked with Vincent. The men were all together, and he felt humbled to be part of such a large family.

"Do you want to go away with me later?" he asked.

"What do you mean?" She looked at him.

During many barbeques they'd been alone. He stared across the yard knowing he couldn't go another night without having her in his arms. "The hotel we were in a few weeks back. We can go there and have some fun." He wanted to sink his fingers into her hair and pull her close.

Holding back the temptation, he sipped at his beer.

"You're wanting to go to the hotel?"

"I want you alone all to myself."

"I don't think that's a good idea. Devil keeps asking questions." She sipped more of her drink. He noticed her nipples were hard buds.

"Let him ask. This is not about him. It's about us." He grew frustrated at not being able to have her all to himself. "Come with me tonight, and I'll fuck you in ways you can't imagine."

"You're driving a hard bargain."

"No, I'm not. You're just playing hard to get."

He reached out to touch her but stopped. Glancing over the garden he saw no one was paying attention to them. "Well, will you be there tonight?"

"Yes. What is this?" she asked, stepping in front of him. Anyone looking their way would think they're having a normal conversation.

"You tell me."

"Am I your dirty little secret?"

Ripper leaned forward, invading her space. "Baby, it's more like I'm *your* dirty little secret. I'd tell Devil any time you're ready."

Seeing Curse watching him, he stood up and stepped around her. "Tonight, pack a bag."

He didn't give her a chance to argue with him as she went to mingle with some of his brothers. Pussy and Death were arguing over stripper duty at the club.

"I'm not going near them. Their claws are going to be the fucking death of me," Pussy said.

Trying to get into the conversation, Ripper struggled to tear his gaze away from Judi. She circled the garden talking with everyone. In the last two years she'd come out of her shell. He felt their time together had helped draw her out even further. She really was a beautiful woman. Lexie came out of the kitchen carrying a tray of ice lollies. Ripper watched Judi grab one, peeling off the wrapper before licking it.

Fuck, his cock thickened at the sight of her plump lips wrapped around the tip sucking it into her mouth. This was torture, pure torture.

"Is something going on between you and the Princess?" Curse asked, stepping up close.

"No, nothing." Tearing his gaze away from the action she was giving the lollie he promised himself he'd make her pay.

His cock was rock hard, and he looked away from his brothers so none of them knew he was struggling with his arousal.

"You'd talk to me if something was bothering you, right?" Curse asked.

"Yeah, sure." He took in several gulps of his beer as he looked around the garden. *Shit, fuck, shit*. He needed to get out of here. He watched Lexie disappear inside. The sound of the telephone ringing could be heard even over the buzz of the garden party.

Devil had his arm wrapped around Judi's shoulders as they talked with Vincent. Phoebe was fingering the bottom of the summer dress she wore. He liked seeing the curve of her legs. She didn't wear any heels. Her legs didn't need them.

He gripped his empty beer bottle watching the ease with which Devil touched her. Ripper couldn't be like that with her. It wasn't easy for him to claim her. He had to have the patience for Judi to make the first move.

Lexie cried out coming toward the door. Her hand was over her mouth as she looked at Devil.

Silence fell over the garden as they stared at each other.

"Everyone, get the fuck out," Devil said, shouting the words out for all to hear.

Ripper watched his guests look at each other in shock. They started moving out of the garden leaving them alone.

He watched as Lexie struggled to keep the news inside as people left. This was club business.

"What the fuck has happened now?" Curse asked.

Glancing at Judi, he saw the fear in her eyes.

"Zero's been shot," Lexie said. Her voice rose for everyone to hear in the garden.

"What? What the fuck are you talking about?" Devil asked, stepping forward.

Ripper saw her hands were shaking.

"There was a drive by shooting. Zero was hit

twice. He's in surgery. Tiny doesn't know if he's going to make it. Angel." Lexie stopped, whimpering.

"What?" Judi asked.

"Angel saw what was about to happen and stepped in front of Zero before Lash could react. She was shot in the back three times. It's a mess, Devil. They need you. There is so much damage." She looked down at the phone as if it was cursed.

Ripper watched as Devil went to her.

"Baby, you can't panic. I will take care of everything. Nothing is going to happen to anyone."

"Angel and Zero have been shot. He said others had as well. Devil, they could die." Lexie sobbed as she threw her hands around her man.

Fisting his hands, Ripper made his way toward Judi. Tears were shining bright in her eyes.

"I like Angel. She's so sweet." He wrapped his arms around her not caring what others thought. She was his woman, and she needed him in those precious moments. Kissing the top of her head, he saw all the men heading inside.

"Tiny wants you to call him back," Lexie said, handing the phone back to him. "It's urgent."

With all of his brothers heading into the house, Ripper cupped her cheek. "Tonight, you'll come to me?" he asked.

"Yes," she said, without hesitation.

Leaving her side, he walked into the house going through to the dining room. He closed the door behind him as Devil put the call through to Tiny.

The phone rang five times before Tiny answered. Over the line, Ripper heard the sadness in Tiny's voice.

"What's going on?" Devil asked.

"The doctors had to sedate Lash. He was tearing up the fucking hospital." Tiny stopped, and there was muttering heard over the line. "He was covered in Angel's blood. Shit, Zero's really in fucking shit."

Ripper listened as Tiny brought them up to speed on the shit that had gone down with Alan. Alan had taken out Angel, and they didn't know if she's going to make it. For the last ten years Zero had been keeping his friend's sister hidden. With the recent news doing the rounds about The Skulls and the damage, this man Alan, the guy Zero was supposed to have killed had resurfaced.

"You don't do anything by half do you, Tiny," Devil said, looking pissed.

"I wouldn't ask for help if it wasn't needed. I've got people dying. Angel, she was a mess, Devil. I can't let this stand even if Zero doesn't make it."

"Fuck, we'll be there."

All the men in the room were in agreement. Ripper wanted to go to Fort Wills and tear apart whoever had dared to hurt his friends. Once Tiny and Devil settled on a date, they hung up.

Arms folded over his chest, Ripper watched as Devil swiped the phone across the room. "Tiny may be the leader of a different MC group, but he is a friend. I won't stand for some fucker thinking they can get the better of us." Devil looked at Ripper. "You'll stay here and keep an eye on our women and the club. I can't go to Fort Wills and worry about Lex. It's not happening. If any of you want to step down then fucking say so now. I'm not in the fucking mood for you acting later."

No one spoke up. Devil looked at each of them. "We'll be riding tomorrow."

****

Judi made her way out of the back of her house the instant she got the text. She knew he'd been busy with club business as Devil and the boys had been locked in his office for a good few hours. Holding onto the brackets she jumped down. Lexie and Devil were in their bedroom. Vincent and Phoebe had taken the kids seeing as this was going to be Devil's last night home for a few weeks.

Tucking her loose hair behind her ear, she made her way out of the back garden and down the road. Ripper was stood at the end of the road without any lights on. He handed her a spare helmet, which she took without question. She didn't like how silent he was being.

Climbing on the back of his bike, she held on tightly to his stomach as he pulled away, riding in whatever direction he wanted. She was nervous about what he was going to say or do.

When the hotel came in sight, she relaxed a little while still holding onto him.

He parked the car up without saying a word. She gave him back the helmet looking toward the reception.

"I've already booked our room." Ripper took her hand, leading her upstairs. She didn't like how quiet he was being with her.

Was he leaving her tomorrow with Devil and the boys?

She went to talk as he opened the door to their room. He stopped her from talking with his lips on top of hers.

Ripper slammed the door closed, pressing her back against the door. His hands were roaming all over her body leaving her in no doubt as to what he wanted to do to her. The hard ridge of his cock pressed to her stomach, making her moan. She would never get used to the thickness of him.

"Fuck, I've been wanting to do that all day." He muttered the words against her lips. "I need to be inside you, baby. Get your clothes off now."

Tearing at her shirt and then her jeans, she watched him revealing his gorgeous body to her.

"What's going on, Ripper?"

"Not right now. I need to be inside you." He stood waiting as she wiggled out of her jeans. She squealed as he tugged her hard, forcing her to trip into his arms. He caught her easily, holding onto her.

Landing on the bed, she moaned as he slid between her thighs. She watched him grip his flesh before rubbing the tip across her clit. Thrusting herself onto his cock, Judi begged him for more. "Please," she said.

"Don't worry, baby. I'm going to give it to you." He moved down to her entrance and slammed in deep.

She felt each pulse of his cock as he jerked inside her. He filled her to the brim. Ripper kissed her nipples while she grew accustomed to the size of his cock.

"You're too big."

His hands gripped her ass, holding her in place as he pulled out only to slam back inside. There was nowhere else for her to go as he pounded her body, fucking her with such force the headboard of the bed smacked the wall.

Judi held onto his shoulders for support. Her orgasm was getting closer with each thrust.

"So fucking juicy." His tongue circled her nipples before he nibbled on the buds. The burst of pain took her by surprise making her gasp at the sudden jolt of pleasure. There was no escaping his passion, and she didn't want to. His strength made her ache for more.

He bit down into her nipple, sucking hard.

Her orgasm crashed through her.

"That's it, baby. Take all of my dick. Make it all nice and wet for me."

She held onto his shoulders for support, trying to

keep herself in one place. The way he was fucking her, she'd go through the wall in a matter of moments if he kept pounding inside her.

Within minutes his cock jerked, and she felt the rush of his cum filling her up. He let out a growl as he filled her with each jet of his sperm. Neither of them spoke for minutes afterwards. The only sound in the room to be heard was the sound of their breathing. She held onto his shoulders, not wanting to let go.

If he was going to Fort Wills, he could die, and the thought of him dying tore her apart.

"I love you," she said, speaking the words aloud.

He gazed down at her. His green eyes were what she thought about late at night when she was alone.

Touching his cheek, she glanced down at his lips, wishing something was different. He stroked her cheek.

"I know we're not promising each other anything, but I thought you should know. I love you, and I've tried not to."

Ripper placed a finger over her lips. "Shut up."

She stopped talking. His cock still filled her, and there was no way for her to escape from his gaze.

"I love you, too," he said.

"No, you don't have to say stuff just because I have." She tried to fight with him.

He caught her hands, holding them against the bed beside her head. She was trapped with no way to get free. "Listen to me, Judi." Ripper moved closer to her face. "I love you. You've tormented me for weeks with how I fucking feel. This is not some easy screw. If I wanted an easy screw I'd fuck Ashley or some of the whores and strippers."

Judi listened to him. Ripper was never going to win awards for saying romantic words.

"I love you, baby, and I'm not going anywhere

else. You're mine, and when Devil gets back into town, I'm telling him about us."

"You can't do that. He'll kill you," she said, panicking.

"I'm doing it. We're not going to be hiding for the rest of our lives. I love you, Judi, and I'm going to lay fucking claim to you. I'm not going through another day of watching him touch you with ease while I can't without fear. You're going to be mine, so stop fucking arguing with me." He slammed his lips down on hers, and she felt his cock stir within her.

Wrapping her arms around his neck, she felt so happy being with him.

"Now, it's time for us to shower, and you're coming with me," he said, picking her up. Ripper lifted her off the bed.

Giggling, she wrapped her legs around his waist as he carried her through to the bathroom. Judi squealed as they both stood underneath the cold spray.

They held onto each other, and she was reminded of what happened this afternoon with The Skulls.

"Are you going to Fort Wills?" she asked.

"No, I'm staying behind to take care of you and Lexie."

Jealousy jolted through her at the mention of Lexie's name. Everyone knew he'd had a thing for her. Judi tensed in his arms at Lexie's name.

"Hey, I wanted Lexie because she was sexy, and I wanted to fuck her. You're everything to me, and I wouldn't give up anything for a chance with her. I would give everything up for you."

Tears filled her eyes. "I never expected anything like this in my life," she said.

He tilted her head back. "You've got a Chaos Bleeds member to fall in love with you, Princess. There's no getting away from it."

She looked up at him as he brushed his lips against hers.

"Devil and some of the boys are going to Fort Wills. I don't know what they're going to do as Zero's in surgery and it's critical." Ripper grabbed the soap and started washing her body. "We're not invincible, and there's only so much we can do."

"I'm pleased you're not going. Angel and Zero got shot that we know of. I don't want anything to happen to you." She held him tightly to her.

He held her close. "Baby, I will not be tamed. I'm staying behind to take care of you. Another time, I'll go and help out my brothers."

She nodded. Judi understood.

They showered together, and throughout it all, she felt happy. When Devil got home they would let the truth of what they'd done out in the open.

Once they were done, she followed him back to the bedroom. They lay down together. His touch was sweet, beautiful, and there was nowhere else she wanted to be than in his arms.

He loves me.

Even with her happiness, Judi knew it wasn't going to be long before they faced a far worse opponent. Devil was not going to take their relationship well. She only hoped he listened to her feelings before he did something he'd regret.

Chapter Twelve

Four days later Ripper stood in Lexie's kitchen watching the women work. They'd gone fruit picking together and were boiling it up for homemade jam. He held onto his cell phone waiting for an update from Devil. Every morning his president phoned to ask about his women and the boys. The first day he phoned, Ripper had been at the club and unable to say what the women were saying. He got earache from the shouting over the line.

He was ordered to stay at the house to keep a constant eye on the women. Ripper felt tormented, knowing his woman was only a few bedrooms down. This was his punishment for not telling Devil what was happening. He stayed in the house and watched his woman every day without being able to touch her.

She was standing at the stove as Lexie added berries to the pot. The whole domestic scene should have terrified him, but it didn't. In fact, he felt humbled and charmed by the two women. The only one who kept his gaze, though, was Judi. Her smile lit up her whole face, filling him with warmth.

Sipping at his coffee, he glanced at Simon and Elizabeth, who were playing in their high chairs.

I could get used to this.

Staring at Judi he imagined her ripe with his son or daughter. Shit, his cock sprang into action at the thought.

"Right, we need to let that boil for a few minutes and then it should be ready to put into the pots we've sterilized," Lexie said, pushing some hair off her face. Her stomach was growing with each day.

"Are you all right? We can stop if you need to take a rest," Judi said, touching Lexie's stomach.

"I'm fine. I'm just worried about Devil. I hate it when he's away. I miss him all the time." There was sadness lurking in her eyes.

"He's fine, Lex. I promise you, Devil will not let anyone kill him," Ripper said.

Judi sent a smile his way, but it didn't reach her eyes.

Later that night Judi sneaked into his bedroom, locking the door behind her.

"What are you doing, baby?" he asked.

"Lexie is down for the night, and I couldn't spend another day away from you." She climbed into bed beside him, wrapping her arms around his waist. "I love you, Ripper."

"I love you, too, baby."

"Are you missing it?" she asked, after being silent for several minutes.

"What?"

"Being with your brothers on the road? Do you miss it?"

Looking up at the ceiling, Ripper thought about it. "Yeah, I miss them. I hate not knowing what's going on. There's only so much I can take over the phone. Devil is always careful with what he says."

"I'll miss you when you have to go." She looked up at him with her chin resting on his chest.

"It's going to be a long time before I leave," he said, smiling.

His hands moved up and down her body, and his cock thickened. She wore a vest top with a pair of small shorts. Her body was flush against his, and he wanted inside her.

Moving out from under her, he rolled her to her stomach and drew her up so her ass was cushioned to his cock. Running his hands up and down her body, he settled on caressing her ass. He really did love her ass. It tempted him in ways an ass really shouldn't.

"You're so fucking perfect, baby."

Tugging the shorts down from her body he found she wasn't wearing any underwear.

She helped him to get them off her body, and he opened her cheeks to stare down at her aching center. The puckered hole of her ass tempted him but nowhere near as much as her pussy.

He pushed the sweats he wore down letting his cock spring forward. The tip was already covered in fluid, and he rubbed the tip through her slit, bumping her clit.

Judi cried out, and he reached forward to cover her mouth.

"Until we tell Devil you can't make too much noise."

She replaced his hands with her own. Satisfied with her silence, he bumped her clit with his cock, pressing two fingers into her soaking wet cunt. Judi was always so wet and needy.

Ripper removed his fingers and slammed his cock deep inside her body. Her screams were muffled by the pillow she placed underneath her head. Keeping her ass cheeks wide, he watched his cock slide into her pussy. She opened up to accept him. "Fuck, baby, you'd go wild if you could see what I see."

Her answer was a moan. Chuckling, he pulled out so only the tip was inside her. He saw her cum coating his cock, and he rammed back inside. In three quick moves he rammed into her, watching her take every inch of his cock.

His fingers were still wet from her cunt, so he slicked them more by caressing her clit. Her pussy tightened around his cock, and he didn't let up until she exploded around his length. Groaning, he paused to relish each clench and spasm of her sweet cunt.

With his slick fingers, he caressed them over her ass. She stayed still while he took his time to play with her ass. There was a time when he loved to share his woman with another member of the Chaos Bleeds crew. He couldn't even imagine sharing Judi. She was his woman, and he didn't want to her with anyone.

"Please, Ripper," she said, begging.

"You like the feel of my cock inside your tight cunt?"

"Yes, please don't stop."

"I'm not going to stop." He pressed a finger to her puckered ass watching the muscles tighten as he sought entry into her ass. "Let me in, baby. I own every inch of you, and that includes your ass."

She whimpered but stayed frozen in place.

"Do you want me in this ass?" he asked.

"Yes." Her voice was only a whisper, but he caught it.

"Then let me inside. I'll give you everything you need. Trust me."

Slowly, Judi began to relax, and he took his time sliding a finger into her ass. She cried out as he pushed to the knuckle. He pumped his finger into her ass several times before adding a second. Her cream soaked his shaft, which was still buried inside her.

"So fucking perfect," he said, gripping her hip with his free hand. She pushed back against him, taking his cock and finger deeper into her ass and pussy. "Good girl. Fuck me back, tell me what you want, and I'll give it to you every chance I get." He tightened his fingers on the flesh of her ass.

"Please, Ripper, you're killing me. Just fuck me."

Gripping one hip he pulled out of her warmth

only to slam back inside. Over and over he fucked inside her, wanting her to forget everything else but his cock. Ripper was relentless as he fucked her, taking her over the edge with his cock alone. He pumped his fingers into her ass, watching her take all of him.

His heart pounded, and Ripper wanted to tell Devil everything. Judi was his, and he wanted a ring on her finger. He already owned the engagement ring he was going to give her. It wasn't conventional, but it was perfect for them.

The moment Judi went over the edge, Ripper slammed deep as the first ripple of his orgasm thrust inside him. He emptied his cum deep into her body, groaning at the pleasure. His blood pumped around his body, and all he could do was moan. Looking down, he saw he'd left fingerprints on her hip from the tightness of his grip. "Shit, baby, you're bruised again."

"When it comes to you, I'm always bruised," she said, looking at him over her shoulder.

Pulling out of her warmth, he placed a kiss to the bruised area and left to grab a cloth. He washed his fingers in the sink then made his way toward her. She was on her knees waiting for him. Ripper cleaned away the mess before throwing the cloth into the laundry basket and grabbed the box from his jacket.

She was sitting on the edge of the bed when he moved toward her. Going to his knees, he opened the box. Inside laid a silver plated ring with a skull on the front. It was one of the rings he wore, and he'd gotten it changed so it would fit her finger.

"Ripper, I don't understand," she said, looking at his ring then at him. "This is one of your favorite rings. You told me you got it on your first year with Chaos Bleeds."

"Judi, you're the love of my life. I can't bear a

moment without you in it." He stopped looking at the ring. "I could get you any old ring that's been made. This is mine, and with you wearing it, everyone will know you're mine." He took the ring out and slid it on his finger. "I want you and the world to know that you're my bitch."

She burst out laughing. "Great, how romantic. I'm your bitch."

He glanced down at the floor. "I've never been good with words and shit, Judi. I can't sell you roses and chocolates and words. What I can give you is myself and my word. I will never back out of either. I love you, and there's no one else I want to spend the rest of my life with. You own me, just as much as I own you." He pointed to his chest. "The moment this is done, I'm getting ink here. 'Property of Judi'."

Tears filled her eyes at his words.

"Fuck, Ripper." She wrapped her arms around his neck. "I don't need sweet words. You're more than enough for me."

****

Two weeks later Judi stood in the clubhouse pinning up the last of the welcome home banners. Devil had called the day before saying they were on their way back. She didn't know how it had gone with The Skulls. Ripper wouldn't say anything other than none of the Chaos Bleeds crew died. She glanced toward the buffet table to see Mia arranging the plates on the table. Ashley had invited the waitress.

Watching the two women, she wondered how they were best friends given their needs. Every time she went to the library, she always ate at the diner. Mia never gave any of the men the time of day. She brushed them off while Ashley loved every single bit of attention. There was no stopping the other woman.

"Ripper's in his room. Will you go and make sure the alcohol is arriving soon?" Lexie asked, coming to stand beside her. Phoebe and Vincent were watching over the kids in the corner of the club. The sweet-butts were ordered to stay on their good behavior. It was going to be one hell of a welcome home party. The only way the club knew how to end their time on the road was by having a party. Judi tucked some hair behind her ear to make her way upstairs. In his bedroom, Ripper was standing without a shirt on looking down at his cell phone. He turned to her, smiling when his gaze landed on her.

"Devil's an hour out. I hope everything is going well downstairs."

"It's going better than you could imagine. Everyone is excited." She closed the door, resting her back to it. On her finger was the ring he'd given her. Judi couldn't take it off. Ripper was such a romantic, and he didn't even know it.

"Are you wanting my cock, baby?" he asked, folding his arms over his chest.

"You stuffed a dildo up my ass at the beginning of this morning and told me to wait for you. I'm bursting at the seams," she said.

Ripper had taken her by surprise when he produced the dildo from his bag of goods. He had taken great pleasure in telling her how much he liked to play with his women. From the bag she knew he'd gone out buying whatever he found with the intention of using it all on her. Now she locked the door and stepped closer.

"You want me to fuck you before everyone turns up." His fingers gripped the back of her neck, drawing her close to him. "Look at those fucking eyes. You're begging to be fucked." He slammed his lips down on hers, taking over. She opened her mouth, waiting for him to take full advantage. Ripper didn't let her down, sliding his tongue deep inside her mouth.

Judi submitted to his touch, loving how he gave her so much pleasure without taking any for himself until she was happy.

"Fuck, I love your lips." He muttered the words against her mouth.

Kissing him back, she gave him pleasure as well.

He dragged her from the center of the room to his bed. Sinking down, she gasped as the fake cock in her ass made its presence known.

"I know how to stop that."

Ripper put her to her knees, dragging up her summer dress then tugging down her panties.

His fingers slid into her pussy as he used his other hand to tease the cock in her ass. He pulled at the dildo, pushing it inside and out driving her wild with need.

"Please, Ripper," she said, begging.

"Don't worry, baby. I'll take care of you." The dildo in her ass was pulled out completely.

She glanced over to see him grabbing something from one of his drawers.

"I've been thinking about this since I put that dildo up inside you." In the next instant she felt the cool gel of the lubricant as he smeared plenty over her. Groaning, she gripped the sheet underneath her as he pressed two fingers inside her, lubing her up.

For several seconds his touch disappeared, and she knew he was preparing his cock.

Taking deep breaths, she tightened her grip on the sheet as he pressed the tip of his cock to her ass.

"I'm going to take my time. Tell me to stop if it hurts too much."

She was burning up from her need. Judi gasped at the sudden burst of pleasure and pain.

"Shh, it's okay, Judi. I'm not going to hurt you."

His voice soothed her as he worked his cock inside her ass.

"Touch your clit. Make it feel good," he said.

Reaching between her thighs, she stroked her fingers through her slit, caressing her clit like he ordered.

The smallest touch had her crying out at the sudden pleasure.

"Yes, please, fuck me, Ripper," she said, wanting to feel him deep into her core.

"That's it, baby. Take all of me."

He pushed his cock into her ass. On the final inch his hands returned to her hips, and he slid all the way inside. "You've got it all. You should see how fucking hot you look with my cock inside your ass. You're all mine, Judi. No one is going to take you away from me."

"I love you, Ripper." She didn't want to go anywhere. The only place she wanted to be was with him.

Ripper pulled out of her only to work his way back inside, going deep. She caressed her clit feeling her orgasm stirring. It never took much for her to explode. Ripper fucked her throughout it all, getting her used to his cock in her ass.

"You're so fucking tight, tighter than your pussy."

She whimpered as his thrusts increased in strength. His hands were once again bruising on her hips. They came together. Her orgasm shooting through her, she thrust back onto his cock, taking him deep.

"Fuck, I love you, baby."

His cock pulsed as he filled her with his cum. Gasping for breath, she collapsed to the bed unable to hold onto her sanity as Ripper took everything. Her body was shaking from need.

"I was going to wait until tonight to fuck you. I just couldn't wait," he said, dropping a kiss to her shoulder.

He pulled out of her body, and she gasped at the sudden feeling of emptiness that claimed her. Ripper came back wiping her ass with a cloth. His touch was so sweet. She smiled up at him, knowing nothing could have gotten better.

She couldn't believe she was in love with Ripper. He was not the kind of man she imagined for herself.

Ripper took his time, cleaning away their lovemaking. Judi was staring into his eyes about to tell him how much she loved him when the door to the bedroom banged open. Jerking up, she saw Devil standing there with Lexie, both staring into the room. Jerking up, Judi let the dress fall down her body. The anger on Devil's face was acute. His face was red, and all that anger was directed at the man she loved.

Glancing at Ripper she saw his jeans rested low on his hips and were unzipped. There was no getting away from what he'd witnessed.

"You fucking perv," Devil said, storming into the room.

Crying out, Judi tried to find her voice, but faced with Devil's anger she couldn't get the words to work.

Devil grabbed Ripper and landed a blow to his face. She was shocked he didn't drop to his knees at the force of the blow.

"Devil, stop," she said, finally finding her voice.

"You fucking perv. I leave you to look after my girls, and you're fucking one of them." Another blow landed to Ripper's face.

Scrambling off the bed, she tried to tug on Devil's arm. He wasn't having any of it. Falling to the bed from being thrown off him, she felt sick.

"It's more than that," Ripper said, getting to his feet. The shouting had brought more of the crew upstairs. She saw Curse standing in the doorway looking at each of them. On the floor lay the dildo that had been thrust up her ass.

"Lexie, stop him," Judi said, getting to her feet.

She watched Devil pull Ripper out of the room. Screaming, she tried to follow them. Lexie caught her, stopping her from moving.

"Baby, you can't follow them. Devil will sort this out. Ripper shouldn't have done what he did."

"No, you don't understand. I love Ripper, and he loves me."

For a pregnant woman, Lexie was incredibly strong holding her at bay.

"Ripper knows the rules. No one is to touch you."

Tears were falling down her cheeks at her words. Curse was looking into the room. "I love him. I wanted his touch. Please, he doesn't want this. I asked him to keep it from Devil." She raised her hand showing the ring he'd given to her. "We're going to get married. Please, he's always been there for me."

"You're the one who killed that guy out on the main road?" Curse asked.

She jerked toward him, shocked. Judi nodded her head.

"You're sure about this?" Lexie asked.

"Yes, I love him. Please, nothing can happen to him."

Chapter Thirteen

The blows were painful, and Ripper doubted he'd be able to see out of one eye by the end of the day. Fuck, this was not how he anticipated Devil finding out the truth. Judi deserved a lot more than this. He heard her screaming, and he only hoped that Devil didn't kill him.

"I love her, Devil," he said.

Another blow came to his eye. Collapsing to the floor, he took the strikes of his foot as he attacked his ribs. He protected himself as best he could. This was what he deserved. No one in their right mind would have touched her.

I love her. Protect her.

"I promised to protect her, and you fuck her. You piece of shit."

He heard her screaming at Lexie to let her go. His brothers were looking at him in a mixture of disgust and sympathy. Ripper took everything, and then the blows stopped as Judi threw herself over him.

"Get away, Judi," he said, not wanting her to risk herself while Devil was gunning for him.

"No, I will not let him kill you."

"Lex, get her out of the way while I end this piece of shit. I trusted him with both of you, and now I'm going to get rid of him like the fucking animal he is." Devil's anger radiated out toward him.

Collapsing in a heap, Ripper accepted everything he gave.

"No, you're not going to kill him. I love him."

Finding the strength, Ripper got to his knees. His jacket was in the bedroom, but he would give everything.

"I love her," Ripper said, moving around her so he was in front of Devil.

Another blow landed to his face, shoving him to

the floor.

"Stop it," Judi said, screaming. "Stop hurting him."

She was picked up out of the way by Pussy. Something kicked in Ripper's mind, and he got to his feet, grabbing Devil's gun from his pocket. "You put her the fuck down now." He turned back to Devil. "I love her. She means everything to me, and I will give up the club to be with her. For her, I will leave, never to return. I will take every beating and come back for more, but I will not give her up."

"You're fucking bluffing," Devil said.

Handing Devil back the gun, Ripper reached out for Judi, tugging her into his arms. "I've asked her to marry me."

Judi lifted her hand up showing everyone the ring. "I said yes. I love him. I don't want anyone but him. Please, stop." She was openly sobbing. "I was the one who told him not to say anything. I love him and will do everything to be with him. If you don't want me around anymore I'll leave with him and be happy doing so."

"Prez," Curse said, gaining his attention. "He covered up one of her kills. I believe him when he says he's in love with her. He's not touched any of the sweet-butts and will not go near any of the women."

The tension could be cut with a knife. Ripper owed Curse far more than he ever thought.

"You're going to marry her?" Devil asked.

"Yes."

"If she didn't demand silence, you would have told me what was going on?"

Ripper nodded, feeling the ache in his ribs. Devil must have cracked some, they hurt that much. "I'm not ashamed to be with her at all. She's my world."

They were silent for several minutes. "Then you

get married today," Devil said, after much silence.

"What?" Judi asked. "We can't get married today."

"You're getting married today, and that's the end of it."

Ripper nodded. "I'll marry her today." He leaned down, kissing her neck.

"You marry today, and everything can be finalized at a later date with the paperwork." Devil took the lead, walking down the stairs. The men, except for Curse, followed behind him. When they were gone, Ripper slumped against the wall, gasping at the pain.

"I'm so sorry," Judi said, cupping his face.

"What do you have to be sorry about?" he asked, holding onto her side.

"If I'd listened to you this wouldn't have happened. Shit, I'm so fucking sorry," Judi said. "Please forgive me."

"Nothing to forgive, babe. Devil was going to kick whoever decided to date you, Judi. I'm just pleased I'm still fucking standing." He coughed, groaning at the sudden jolt of pain.

"You're barely fucking standing at the moment," Curse said, handing him a jacket.

Coughing, he took the jacket and slowly slipped it on.

"I'll give the doctor a call to bind those ribs up," Curse said, moving away.

"Thanks, man, for having my back."

"I wouldn't have helped you if I didn't know you were telling the truth." Curse left.

Judi looked ready to burst into tears again. "You don't have to marry me if you don't want to."

Taking hold of her hand, he dropped a kiss to the ring he'd given her.

"My only regret is you're not going to get the white wedding you deserve. I'd marry you in a fucking field so long as I got to stay by your side." He kept hold of her hand and used the wall to keep him on his feet.

Downstairs, Devil had a minister waiting. The guy looked petrified, but Ripper was not going to back away. He wasn't lying, and he'd prove it. He loved Judi and would give his life to be with her.

She held onto his shoulder, not letting go as they made their way downstairs together. Judi's hands kept him steady. Together, they walked down toward the rest of the club. Standing in front of the minister, Ripper spoke the words, and then Judi did, binding their lives together.

Once it was all over, he kissed her lips, and the room cheered and threw their hands up in celebration.

When the minister was gone, Devil walked up to him with Lexie beside him.

"I had every intention of killing you, Ripper," he said. "You make her sad or think of looking at another woman and you will find yourself six feet under."

"I've got everything I want right here," Ripper said, tugging Judi to his side.

"She's still living in my house until college is finished. You can look for a place to live, but you're staying in the spare bedroom and I will lock you in it. I don't want any fucking in my house."

Lexie slapped Devil on the arm. "Leave them alone. This was their makeup wedding. I can't believe you made them do this today. You can see they're in love."

Ripper let Judi go for Lexie to hug her. Staring into Devil's eyes, he saw the nod outside. Kissing Judi's temple he made his way outside, trying to ignore the pain with every step he took.

In the outside surrounded by privacy, Ripper waited for the blow that was likely to come. When Devil turned to face him, he was shocked there was no gun pointed at him. "You protected Judi?"

"Yes. She was out one night, and one of her old clients tried to pick her up. She shot him."

"Where did you bury the body?"

Ripper gave him the location.

"I'm calling Jerry. He was looking for the man you described, and he can handle it from here." For several minutes Devil took care of business leaving Ripper to wait.

He was married, or close to being married.

Smiling, he looked up at the shining sun. He was married and in love.

"You love her, don't you?"

"She's my world."

Devil nodded. "I see her as a daughter, and if this was not what I think it is, then you'd be dead. I'll give Judi everything. I don't care if we don't have the same blood, but I know you'll take care of her and love her."

"I will. I'll take care of looking for a house. I don't want her living in the clubhouse."

"Fuck, what has happened to us? We fucked everything in sight, and now we're all settling down. Just like The Skulls." Devil shook his head.

"What happened in Fort Wills?" Ripper asked.

"A lot of shit that you don't need to hear on your wedding day. Tiny knows what he's doing, and we've helped where we can. The rest of the shit is up to them." Devil slapped him on the back. "Take care of the Princess."

"I never meant to hurt you or the club," Ripper said, staring at the ground as Devil moved away. "I was tormented with my feelings, and I fought them. Judi, she's hard to ignore."

"She's in love with you, Ripper. Make it worth her while to be with you."

He watched Devil go wishing there was something else he could say. Going inside the clubhouse, he went with the doctor to check over his aches and pains. Judi stayed with him, clearly concerned for his wellbeing.

Holding onto her hand, he made a note to get her a wedding band and also to get the appointment for the new ink on his chest.

"You're insane," Judi said, caressing his cheek.

"Baby, we're together. I don't care what you think." He kissed her temple feeling calm for the first time in his life.

****

Five months later

Judi licked her lips as the honey drizzled down her chin. She had dipped some strawberries into honey and was eating them while waiting for Devil and Ripper to get back from the clubhouse. Gazing down at the ring on her finger she got a buzz knowing she was properly married. The papers were signed a month after they were married at the clubhouse. Once the papers were done, they had another small ceremony at the clubhouse, this time a planned one. She was allowed to wear her white dress even though she wasn't in the church.

Churches were overrated.

"You're looking happy," Lexie said, carrying her newborn through to the kitchen. A couple of weeks ago Lexie had given birth to a beautiful bouncing baby boy. Simon and Elizabeth were loving it, and Lexie looked happier than she ever had before.

"I am. Devil and Ripper will be back from the club any minute now."

"What's with the strawberries and honey?" Lexie asked.

"I thought it would be healthier than double cream, and the strawberries are too tart." She offered one to Lexie who declined.

"No thanks." There was a smile on her face that had Judi suspicious.

"What are you hiding?" Judi asked.

"Nothing that won't be known in a few hours."

For the last five months she and Ripper had to steal a little time here and there together. If it wasn't other members of the club keeping an eye on them it was Devil or Lexie. They hadn't slept together in five months at Ripper's request. The moment the ring went on her finger, Devil accepted their relationship and backed off. The only problem Devil had was the living arrangements. He wouldn't allow her to leave his home until he was satisfied Ripper had a house ready for the pair of them. She wasn't allowed to stay at the club unless it was for parties.

Judi wasn't going to argue, and she was more than happy with the new arrangement. But she'd been so shocked when Ripper refused to have sex with her. She was surprised he hadn't exploded from all the times she tried to get him to cave. Judi knew she couldn't take much more. Ripper was not supposed to be this nice but demand sex. Her body was on fire with need for his cock. Ripper was allowed to stay at the house, and he stayed in her bedroom, which surprised her with Devil's daddy role still firmly in place. Judi was so desperate for release she'd even asked Devil to have a word with him for Ripper to give in. Nothing.

College was nowhere near finished, but she'd done plenty of reading in the last five months seeing as Ripper wouldn't occupy her time in the bedroom. He actually asked for her to read him some of her assignments.

She thought Ripper's sudden conservative behavior was ridiculous. When she confronted him about it, he smiled, cupped her cheek, and gave her the best kiss she'd ever experienced to shut her up. He was planning something. She didn't know what it was, but there were plenty of times she'd walk into a room where he'd be talking with Devil showing him stuff on his phone or from a file and that file would disappear when she started asking questions.

"You're keeping something away from me?" she asked.

"Honey, I promise you, you'll love it," said Lexie.

"I doubt it." She muttered the words so Lexie wouldn't hear them.

An hour later Ripper walked inside the house going to her and tugging her in his arms. "Hey, baby, I've missed you." He deepened the kiss. She moaned, wrapping her arms around his neck as he plunged his tongue deep into her mouth.

"Enough," Devil said. "My son is watching, and I don't want him getting any ideas while looking at you two."

Laughing, she pulled away wishing she didn't have to let go at all. Ripper's arms stayed around her as she continued to eat her strawberries and honey.

Devil had kept an eye on her wanting to know if she was pregnant. The very thought of being pregnant filled her with dread.

"Can we go?" Ripper asked.

"Sure, I'll see you on Monday."

Judi frowned, looking from Ripper to Devil.

"Pack a bag, honey. We've got a place to go. I

told you it was going to be special."

She didn't need to be told twice. Running up to her room, she quickly threw items into a bag before going back downstairs.

Devil and Lexie saw them outside. Climbing on the back of Ripper's bike, she held on tightly. They were riding for a good twenty minutes before he pulled up outside of a house. She watched him type in a code into a security system, and the gates opened.

Keeping her thoughts to herself, she looked up at the large house. It wasn't as large as Devil's, but it was comfortable.

Climbing off, she handed Ripper her helmet. "Where are we?" she asked.

He covered her eyes and moved her toward the door.

"What's going on?" She started laughing as Ripper kissed her neck.

"Stop spoiling my fun."

The sound of the door opening and a light being flicked were easily heard. Several more steps were taken, and then the door behind her closed.

"This is kind of freaking me out," she said.

He released her eyes and told her to open them. Glancing around, she looked at the house.

"What is this?"

She took a step into each room seeing the sitting room, which only held one chair. Going through the back to the kitchen to see minimal items on the counters, she loved it instantly.

"This is our home," he said.

Turning to face him, she found him leaning against the doorframe.

"What?"

"This is our home. I wanted a place to call our

own. This is it. Do you like it?"

Judi looked around the room, feeling excited. "This is our home?"

"Yes."

"You're not going to stop me kissing you or asking for more?"

"No, I'm not. This is our place, and I've not touched you or done anything with you as I wanted our first time after our marriage to be special. Devil is my boss, and I respect him. I'm not going to screw his daughter under his roof while he's there. It's tacky. I wanted something for us, to call our own," he said. "When you wake up in the morning, I want you to be free to come down here naked if you want."

Running toward him, she threw herself into his arms. "Then take me to bed before the fun comes to an end."

The last five months had been a nightmare for her. It was the first time in her life when she really craved his touch. Ripper hadn't lost his place in the club for being with her, but he had to prove to them he was being serious about them. He didn't touch another woman, and she was starting to trust him more with each passing day.

Ripper started laughing. "This is our home. We're going to have to furnish it, and you need to finish college, but everything is good in the club. They accept us, baby."

Wrapping her arms around his neck, she drew him down for a kiss.

"I don't care if they're not going to turn up. Please, Ripper, take me upstairs and make love to me. I'm going to explode if you don't."

He kissed her lips, chuckling at her growl of annoyance.

"Come on then, baby. It's time for you to see our bedroom." He lifted her up in his arms, carrying her up the flight of stairs to the third bedroom along the corridor.

She held on tightly as he kicked the door open, dropping her to the bed. Moaning, she claimed his lips as he sank between her thighs. They tore at their clothing until nothing was between them.

Judi opened her thighs, loving the feel of his cock stretching her.

"I love you, Judi. You own my heart, and this is going to be something you'll never forget."

Pressing a finger to his lips she smiled up at him. "Shut up and fuck me."

He plunged inside her, making her cry out with pleasure. There was nowhere else she wanted to be. She hadn't believed it was possible to fall in love, but Ripper made everything possible to her.

Epilogue

Curse sat at the diner flicking through the menu trying to think of something to eat. Lexie had already fed him that morning after a club meeting at Devil's house, but still he came to the diner to eat.

"Can I get you anything?" Mia asked, holding a pot filled with coffee.

"I'll have a cup of your finest," he said, smiling.

Ripper and Judi were at the library while she did more studying, and Curse had opted to come here. He couldn't help it. Every time he left the diner after getting his fill of Mia, he promised himself it would be his last time. She never showed an interest in him at all. In fact, she never showed any interest in any of the club members. She was always busy working at the diner or looking after her mother.

Everything he found out about her had come from her best friend, Ashley. The two women were like chalk and cheese, and yet they were the best of friends. He didn't understand it. Ashley loved sex, men, and partying. Mia loved taking care of people.

"Where is Ashley?" Mia asked, pouring some hot coffee into his mug. All thought left his mind as she smiled.

Fuck, Ashley. She wants to know where Ashley is. Thinking, he knew she'd spent the night with Pussy.

"She's, erm, she's busy," he said, feeling his cheeks heat.

Mia giggled. "She's with a man." She shook her head, placing her palm on his arm. "Don't worry about it. I can see Ashley when she's free."

"How on earth are you two friends?" he asked.

Her smile dropped as sadness filled her eyes. "We've always got each other's backs. She's there when

I need her to be."

He noticed her hands started to shake.

Suspicion filled him at her reaction. After many years of having to deal with guilty men, he knew the signs.

"Let me know when you're hungry. I'll bring you some food."

She left him alone as Ripper and Judi joined him.

The two lovebirds made him feel sick. At least Judi wasn't pregnant and temperamental. She was a sweet thing.

Picking up his coffee, he drowned out the conversation watching the curvy woman who'd been invading his thoughts. He wanted to know all of her secrets, and he was going to find them out.

The End

www.samcrescent.com

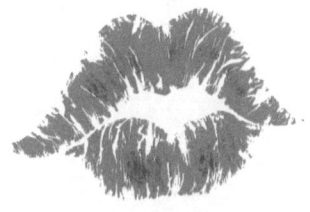

EVERNIGHT PUBLISHING ®

www.evernightpublishing.com